Lucy was like a little sister to him. . . except she wasn't.

Lucy was just a kid…except she wasn't anymore. Lucy didn't want him to kiss her…except she was swaying toward him, and her gaze was fixed on his mouth as if she were willing it to come closer to hers.

Carlo found himself moving nearer.

Was he really this weak? Apparently he was. Or the attraction was just that strong.

Now was the last chance to dredge up his common sense, to gather his brain cells together, to do *something* rather than give in.

Lucy swallowed again. "What would it take for me to get a bite of that pie?"

His laugh was low. "I'm sure we can think of something."

She didn't move as he took the fork out of her unresisting hand and set it on the table. She didn't blink as he drew her against him. And she didn't make a sound as he finally succumbed to temptation and lowered his mouth to taste hers.

Dear Reader,

Like me, the heroine of this book, Lucy Sutton, would prefer to avoid roller coasters. She knows it doesn't take an amusement-park ride to get her pulse racing and her heart thumping—her temporary boss can give that to her with just one look from across the office!

But it's Carlo Milano who really needs to get away from his desk and into the sunshine, and Lucy will do what she must to make that happen. He's an old family friend after all...as well as the crush she's hidden for years.

I love office romances and watching a girl *finally* get her man—*Bachelor Boss* offers both! I hope you enjoy it as much as I enjoyed telling Carlo and Lucy's story.

Christie Ridgway

BACHELOR BOSS

CHRISTIE RIDGWAY

SPECIAL EDITION®

Published by Silhouette Books
America's Publisher of Contemporary Romance

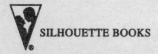

SILHOUETTE BOOKS

ISBN-13: 978-0-373-24895-7
ISBN-10:   0-373-24895-4

BACHELOR BOSS

Books by Christie Ridgway

Silhouette Special Edition

Beginning with Baby #1315
From This Day Forward #1388
**In Love with Her Boss* #1441
Mad Enough to Marry #1481
Bachelor Boss #1895

Silhouette Desire

His Forbidden Fiancée #1791

Silhouette Yours Truly

The Wedding Date
Follow That Groom!
Have Baby, Will Marry
Ready, Set...Baby!
Big Bad Dad
The Millionaire and the Pregnant Pauper
The Bridesmaid's Bet

*Montana Mavericks: Home for the Holidays

CHRISTIE RIDGWAY

is a native Californian and a born romantic. Her babysitting money was all spent on red licorice and Harlequin romance novels, which makes it all the sweeter to now be writing love stories herself!

A *USA TODAY* bestselling author, she lives in Southern California with her three heroes—her husband and two sons. Visit her Web site at www.christieridgway.com.

To all the little sisters out there who were never taken as
seriously as they should have been—
not that I know anything about that!

Chapter One

Lucy Sutton disliked first days.

Standing before the half-open door leading to her new boss's office, Lucy admitted to herself that in truth she *hated* first days. As family legend had it, she'd hidden at the back of her closet on the first day of kindergarten. While that wasn't clear in her memory, she could recall in vivid detail the first day of high school, the way the tag on her new shirt scratched the back of her neck, how she'd scratched at her nerve-induced hives. The worst, however, was the first day of a new job. Without a mother's hand to hold or a gaggle of girlfriends with whom to get through the hours, that initial eight-to-five at a new place of employment could be excruciating.

Which didn't help explain why Lucy had put herself

through quite a few of *those* new days since graduating from college with an accounting degree three years before.

Swallowing to ease her dry mouth, she reminded herself that despite how her employers had liked her and her work, each of those three number-crunching jobs had not been quite right for her. Still, she knew that more than one of her relatives thought it was *Lucy* who wasn't right for successful employment. That was family legend, too, that Lucy, nicknamed "Lucy Goosey" thanks to one of her ultraperfect elder siblings, was just too flighty and too fluffy to take anything seriously—or to be taken seriously by anyone.

Worst of all, though, was how legends like those had an uncomfortable way of becoming fact.

"Not that legend," Lucy murmured to herself, steeling her spine and scratching at a rising bump on her left wrist. "This time I'm going to show every other Sutton that I'm as capable as they are." This job would be different.

Even though it was only temporary secretarial work, she'd stick with it and succeed. Then she'd move on to finding the very best place for herself and her accounting skills. The right position was out there and this was her stepping stone to it.

Her gaze slid over to the nameplate on the wall beside her new boss's office door. Carlo Milano. She had something to prove regarding him, too.

Specifically, that she was over him.

Taking a deep breath, she rapped gently on the grained wood.

"Come in," a man's voice called out.

Lucy found herself hesitating, and instead of moving forward she thought back to the last time she'd seen Carlo. It had been at a big do a couple of years before at her sister, Elise's, home. He'd been making one of his rare appearances, leaning his rangy, six-foot-two body against a wall in a corner of the kitchen, dressed casually in jeans and a button-down shirt. Yet he'd looked anything but casual, his incredible face serious and leaner than ever, as if any soft and approachable thing about him had been pared away.

Pared away by heartaches she knew he wouldn't speak of.

Oh, she'd attempted to lighten his mood that night. Nobody ever said Lucy wasn't one to bring fun to a party. But after trying to get a laugh—she would have settled for a smile!—out of him with an amusing story about an old roommate, Carlo had merely shaken his head.

"Goose," he'd said gently—yes, he'd actually called her *Goose*—"Use your pretty smiles and your charming wiles on someone who'll appreciate them."

Then Carlo had drawn his knuckle down the side of her suddenly heating cheek. In response, and on impulse—another of her weaknesses according to family lore—Lucy had risen to tiptoe and tried one last thing to give Carlo a little jolt of life by brushing her mouth against his.

Seven hundred and thirty-four nights had passed since then, and her lips still burned at the memory.

Her pride still smoldered around the edges, too—because within seconds Carlo had pushed her away and left his corner…never to be seen by her again.

Until now.

"I said 'come in.'" Carlo's almost impatient-sounding voice interrupted her reverie.

Showtime, she thought, and with one last stroke of right-hand fingernails against her itchy left wrist, Lucy walked into the office.

Her breath caught.

Carlo's massive desk stood in front of her, the leather chair behind it empty, but the wall behind that—ah, that was really something, a whole expanse of glass that revealed a spectacular view of San Diego Bay. It looked like a huge, ten-by-twenty-foot postcard, in which Crayola sky-blue met grayer-blue waters dotted with sailboats and motorboats and yachts. The watercrafts' movement created frothy, egg-white trails across the Pacific's surface and was the only proof they were actually moving and not just part of a lifelike painting titled *Stupendous Southern California.*

It was a multimillion-dollar view that made clear to Lucy that Carlo Milano, longtime family friend and former cop, had struck gold in his high-priced and highly regarded events security business. Obviously he was busy enough to need her to fill in for his secretary for the next three weeks. The man who was her new— albeit temporary—boss had done well for himself.

But where *was* the man who was now her boss?

From the corner of her eye she caught movement at the far end of the room, beyond a spacious seating area that included a love seat, coffee table, two chairs and a built-in bar. A man in a dark jacket was standing there, his back half-turned to Lucy, his attention on a woman in an exquisite, powder-blue suit with matching sling backs. Shiny, pin-straight hair fell in a bright chestnut waterfall toward her waist.

The nape of Lucy's neck burned and new hives popped out on her arms. Her hand reached up to finger the ends of her own wheat-colored, wavy hair. In her beige heels, khaki skirt and plain white blouse, she'd never felt so, well…washed-out.

And so like a third wheel. The pointy toes of Little Blue Suit's little blue shoes were just inches from the toes of Carlo's cordovan loafers, and the beautiful woman looked one breath away from latching on to his mouth.

What should Lucy do now? Interrupt the moment?

Surely not. Surely it would be better to backpedal out of the office. A woman who wanted—no, needed—to succeed at this job should go back to her desk. A woman who needed—and yes, wanted—to prove to herself she was over her unrequited crush on her boss should do nothing to bar the man from getting lucky.

Or from Carlo getting kissed. She should be happy for him as she snuck away. That's what a grown-up, dignified, over-the-infatuation woman would do.

Grown-up, dignified, over-the-infatuation Lucy heard her throat clear. Not too loudly. But loud enough that her presence couldn't be avoided or ignored.

Argh. How could she have done something so intrusive? Now Carlo wasn't going to be pleased. Now she wasn't feeling the least bit adult and dignified during her first moments on the first day of this new job. And then she heard herself make that attention-demanding, throat-clearing sound again.

Carlo's head turned. He looked her way. "Hey."

Lucy's heart wobbled. There it was, that handsome face she'd never forgotten, those dark eyes taking her in. She couldn't read their expression. Displeasure? Or was that relief?

She wiggled her fingers in return greeting. "Hey." She hoped she looked more together than she felt. Dignified, remember? Adult. But…but…*Carlo about to be kissed by someone else!* Did her weird reaction to that show on her face? "I'm sorry, but you, um, you told me to come in and…"

"No problem." He was moving away from the woman in the teensy suit. Her expression was annoyed, but Carlo didn't appear to be the least affected, let alone angry that Lucy had interrupted his tête-à-tête. If a kiss had been in the offing, he didn't seem worried about the missed opportunity.

Her spirits lifted a little. Maybe this particular first day wasn't going to be too bad, despite her fears. As a matter of fact, Carlo *did* look somewhat pleased as he came toward her. See? It was all good. He didn't appear aware of that little crush she'd once had on him. He may not even recall that impulsive lip-lock she'd laid on him herself two years ago.

Though his nonreaction at the time had only added to her embarrassment, now she was grateful that he seemed to have forgotten it. Yes, in his eyes at this minute she must appear dignified, not to mention all of her twenty-five grown-up years. She took his attitude as an omen for her upcoming job success.

"Damn," he said as he came to a stop in front of her.

His long arm reached out to muss her hair the way an uncle would do to a favored young niece. "Long time no see, Goose."

Apparently if she hadn't interrupted a smooch between Carlo and Little Blue Suit, it would have been a kiss-off kind of kiss, anyway. At least that's what he intimated to Lucy—"Please, Carlo, no one calls me Goose anymore," she'd said firmly—when, after ushering his chestnut-haired guest from the office, his first request as her brand-new boss was to ask her to send two dozen roses to the lady who'd just departed. Recipient: a Ms. Tamara Maxwell. Message line: *It wasn't you, it was me.*

He didn't quite meet her eyes when he imparted that interesting nugget, but muttered as he turned back to his office, "Look, we only went out a few times and she didn't get it. I don't do the couple thing."

Lucy got it. She'd always gotten it, though the knowledge had never seemed to cool the particular thing she had for Carlo. Besides the paycheck, putting out that fire for good had been the most pressing reason to accept the job at his company.

When she'd moved back to San Diego, her dad, who was old friends with Carlo's dad, suggested she fill the temporary position at McMillan & Milano before she started a serious search for an accounting position in town. It was supposed to be a favor to Carlo, but it worked for Lucy, too. Moving back to California from Arizona had left her strapped for cash, and acting as his secretary would solve another lingering problem.

The way she figured it, three weeks at McMillan & Milano would finally, for-once-and-for-all, extinguish what she'd always felt for him.

Heck, she decided, watching him walk away from her without a second glance and remembering how easily her humiliatingly juvenile nickname had tripped off his tongue, by quitting time today her libido should finally have heard the message. There was no hope. Carlo would never look at her with the kind of heat a man should hold for a woman.

The idea didn't depress her in the least.

Really.

So she went about her duties, finding this office not so different from any other—including walking into the break room in the late afternoon to find the water cooler drained desert-dry. Stacked on the floor beside it were several full, capped bottles.

"'Water, water, everywhere, but not a drop to drink,'" Lucy murmured, paraphrasing Coleridge to the empty room. She hadn't *just* crunched numbers at school. Shaking her head, she pushed up the cuffs of her sleeves. Even though she wasn't the one who'd tapped the last of the liquid, everyone knew first-day employees couldn't leave the rest of the staff waterless.

No matter that at five foot two and a mere few orders of French fries over her ideal weight, it would be a struggle to replace the bottle. The task was still up to Lucy.

The empty one was a snap to lift away from the top of the water cooler. The blue cap on the closest full bottle took only seconds to peel off. Then, staring down the plastic barrel at her feet as if it were a wrestling opponent, she bent her knees to grasp it around its cool, rotund belly. As she straightened, she staggered on her feet, her heels clattering against the smooth hardwood floor.

Oh, Lord, don't let me drop this.

"Goose, what are you doing?"

Instinct had her swinging toward the voice—Carlo's voice—but that only made her more unsteady on her business-beige heels. Before she could do more than wheeze, there were a man's arms around her—Carlo's arms. Her back was up against his chest, her butt pressed to his—

"Stop," he ordered into her ear.

"I wasn't thinking anything!"

"Obviously not. You're too small to take care of this. I meant 'stop trying to help.' Let go and let me have the bottle."

"Oh." She dropped her hands from the heavy plastic, but that still left her in the circle of Carlo's arms. His warmth was at her spine, his delicious aftershave in her nose, his breath stirring the hair at her temple.

As a wild rash of prickly awareness broke out like more hives over her skin, she dipped under his arm and freed herself from his faux embrace. Without a glance at her, he stepped forward to flip the bottle on top of the cooler.

He turned to find her fanning her face.

"Goo— Lucy…" His voice trailed off as his gaze dropped lower. His eyes widened, then he looked back up. "You, uh, have a couple of buttons that came loose."

She glanced down, gasped. In her struggles with the

water bottle, apparently some of the buttons on her all-business blouse had popped free, revealing most of her white lace demibra. Her face burning, she clutched the shirt's edges together with one hand while hastily re-fastening with the other.

"Relax," Carlo said. "It's just me."

"Yeah. Just you," Lucy repeated.

Just the man she'd dreamed about since she was fifteen years old.

She managed to get decent once more, but was still struggling with the top buttonhole when her new boss made a brotherly noise and moved in as she continued to fumble. "Here. Let me finish it up."

He was wearing an easy, indulgent smile as he pushed her hands away and reached toward her collar. For an instant, his fingertips brushed the hollow at her throat and she jerked in helpless reaction, her pulse pounding against his touch. He froze, his fingertips now only making contact with button and fabric.

Still, his nostrils flared and she could smell her perfume rise around them, the scent surging stronger as her heart continued to hammer in her chest.

He cleared his throat. "Goose," he said. "You smell like a girl."

A nervous bubble of laughter escaped her throat. "Carlo, I *am* a girl."

"Right. Yeah." He made quick work of the stubborn top button, then retreated toward the doorway. There, he shoved his hands in his pockets and cocked his head, studying her. "Actually, you're more than a girl. You're a woman."

"You noticed?" If it hadn't been obvious before, this little comment made it crystal clear that the kitchen-kiss two years before hadn't even rated his attention.

He leaned one shoulder against the jamb and gave her a half smile. "Now I think I'll find it hard to forget."

The deep note in his voice stroked like a brush down Lucy's spine, bumping against each vertebrae. Her tongue swiped at her dry bottom lip and she watched his eyes follow the movement.

Suddenly, her heart sped up again, her pulse fluttering against the place at her throat that still throbbed from his accidental touch. Was...was Carlo looking at her with a masculine kind of interest?

She took in the gleam in his deep-set, dark eyes and then tried to find more clues in the aquiline line of his masculine nose and the sensual curve of his full mouth. He was a beautiful man, every artistic angle of his face a testament to his Italian heritage—but she couldn't read his expression.

She licked her bottom lip again.

Carlo abruptly straightened, his gaze dropping away. "So, uh, Goose—"

"Lucy." And didn't that answer her question? No man would feel the least bit of lust for someone he thought of as "Goose." Disappointment coursed through her, even though she'd taken the job for this— to finally accept there was no mutual heat between her and Carlo.

No heat. No hope.

"So, *Lucy,* I suppose I should get back to work."

With an inward sigh, she followed him with her gaze

as he strode down the hall, admiring the way the European cut of his pale blue dress shirt accentuated the muscled leanness of his back and waist. She didn't try to find a word for how she felt about the curve of his tight, masculine behind in the dark slacks.

Three weeks, Lucy. Three weeks to look, but not touch. Three weeks to accept, finally, that's all you'll ever have of him.

A few minutes before five, she was congratulating herself on making it through the could-be-disastrous initial day, when a messenger appeared with a high-priority package for Carlo. Fine, she thought, she'd deliver the slender cardboard envelope and bid him good-night at the same time. Then her first day on the job, and her first day with Carlo, would be behind her.

At her tap on his door, he called her inside. This time he was sitting behind his desk, file folders in front of him, his computer screen angled just so.

He looked up as she entered. "Lucy. Just the person I've been thinking about all afternoon," he said, leaning back in his chair.

Her fingers squeezed the package. "Me?" The view behind him was still awe-inspiring, but she couldn't drag her gaze away from his face to appreciate it. He'd been thinking about her?

"I realize I don't know what brought you back to San Diego."

"Oh." What to say? Dissatisfaction with the jobs she'd found in the accounting industry she'd spent four years preparing herself for? It made her sound so flighty. So, well…ditzy and goosey, especially when every Sutton sibling had gone straight from graduation to climbing the ladder of success in the corporations they'd joined right after college. "Of course, you know I'm from here, and…"

"Your father mentioned something to mine about disappointments in Phoenix?"

She shifted her weight on her feet. "Well…um…" Her face was heating up again and she didn't know what more to say. While she knew the jobs in Phoenix had not been quite right for her, would Carlo, like her family, only see her as unable to settle down?

"I got to thinking you might have had man trouble."

Lucy blinked. Man trouble? The only man trouble she'd had recently was the trouble she had forgetting about Carlo and the feelings for him she couldn't seem to stamp out. "It's not—"

"I admit that until just a couple of hours ago I was still picturing you at about fourteen years old in my mind. Banged-up knees, a mouthful of braces and all those white-gold curls."

Terrific. While she'd been tossing and turning at night, wondering what it would be like to be with him, his lingering image of her was something that sounded horribly close to Pippi Longstocking.

Carlo cleared his throat. "But now I see that you're all grown-up. Like I said earlier, a woman."

Hmm. That sounded more interesting. And even more interesting than that was the way he was staring at her mouth again. Could it be…?

Uncertain, Lucy held her breath as the atmosphere in the room seemed to ripple with a new, tingly charge.

He jerked his gaze from her mouth to her eyes. "And I was thinking maybe you're here because someone broke your heart."

"Oh. No. N-not yet." Because so far she hadn't quite accepted she could never have Carlo. And now, with this new shimmer of tension in the room, she was even less sure it could never be.

No, Lucy. No! Don't delude yourself!

Listening to her common sense, she interrupted the drift of the conversation by sliding the priority envelope in front of him. "Anyway, this just came for you. It looks important."

When he picked it up, she turned. "I'll see you tomorrow, Carlo."

"Wait."

She didn't spin back around. "It's after five."

"But we're old friends, and I was thinking that since you're doing me the big favor of filling in—" His voice broke off. *"Damn."*

Curiosity reversed the direction of her feet. "You were thinking…?"

He was staring down at what looked to be a pair of tickets in his hands. "I was thinking, no, I *know*," he said, grimacing, "that I could use a date for tonight."

Lucy swallowed. "Is there someone you'd like me to get on the phone for you? Tamara, or…?"

"You, Lucy."

"Me?" She was beginning to sound like an echo machine.

Carlo was up and around his desk before she could run for the door. Not that she really wanted to. Not when he came close enough to do up her buttons again…or undo them.

The air was jittering with tension. And heat. Or maybe that was just her. No. *No.* Carlo was standing over her and she saw his nostrils flare as he took in another breath of her perfume. He was looking at her in a manner that surely he wouldn't waste on Pippi Longstocking.

You smell like a girl.

I see that you're all grown up.

A woman.

"So will you go with me to a party tonight?" he asked.

She curled her fingernails into her palms. "Oh, well…"

"I can introduce you around. Maybe find you—"

"The man I've been missing?" Lucy couldn't say what made her utter the words. They came out of nowhere, sounding a little hoarse, a little flirty, a little like she was flirting with *him.*

She felt both appalled and excited. Outside of a few jokes and that one humiliating kiss, she'd never been overt when dealing with him.

Carlo's brow lifted, and a corner of his mouth ticked up, too. One of his fingers reached out to wrap itself around a lock of her hair. He tugged. "Lucy. Is that what you're looking for?"

Her tongue trailed across her bottom lip and she lowered her lashes—again in what seemed a totally un-thought-out, yet obviously flirty way—to gaze at him through them. "It depends on how far I'll have to go to find him."

Carlo shook his head, an amused, masculine smile quirking both corners of his mouth. "My, my, my. You *have* grown up."

Enough to know what this was. No mistaking it now. Carlo was looking at her with a new kind of interest, with the sort of heat she'd only fantasized about before. Her blood raced through her body, waking up thousands of nerve endings with the thrilling news.

Carlo's looking at me the way a man looks at a woman!

His knuckle ran down her cheek and she felt it all the way to her toes. "Eight o'clock," he said. "Cocktail attire."

"Yes." *Yes, yes, yes!*

"Where shall I pick you up?"

The racing movement of Lucy's blood stopped, stilling in one fell *swoosh*. That shimmering heat continued between them, but she wondered for just how long.

"Where, Lucy?"

"My sister's. Until I find my own place, I'm staying with Elise."

And then Lucy had her answer. The tension, the temperature, the thread of attraction running between them didn't last even another moment, instead dropping like an anchor from one of the boats traveling through the bay she could see over his shoulder. She leveled her gaze at the pretty sight, even as she noted the unpretty view of Carlo's expression closing down.

His hand dropped, his feet stepped away. "I'll be there at eight."

He didn't renege on the invitation. Former cop, old family friend that he was, he wouldn't be out-and-out rude to her. Even if it meant picking Lucy up at the home of her married sister.

Her sister. The unrequited love of Carlo Milano's life.

Chapter Two

There was a rap on the door of the guest bedroom as Lucy stood before the open closet, frowning. "Come in."

Her sister stuck her head inside the room. "Dad called while you were in the shower. He wanted to know how your first day went."

"I hope you told him I haven't quit," Lucy said. "And I didn't get fired, either," she continued, muttering under her breath. Though not true, she suspected that was what her family had assumed each time she'd changed jobs.

Her grumble caused a frown to mar her sister's perfect face as she stepped into the bedroom and swung the door shut behind her. "Are you okay?"

Lucy avoided a probing gaze by turning back to the

closet. "Cocktail attire. For an advance party to hype the Street Beat rock music festival at the end of the month. Don't you think that calls for something a bit less conservative than a little black dress?"

"I don't know," Elise replied, coming to stand beside her. "You're the music lover. Carlo was smart to invite you."

"Yeah. Smart." Lucy figured it was more out of convenience than IQ. Carlo had needed a date for the business thing and she'd been the closest available woman. Those short moments of self-delusion when she'd thought her fantasies had come true...well, self-delusion said it all. "Since I'm working for him, I thought I'd better say yes. Though I'm sure he has a black book full of numbers he could have called."

"He dates. I know that."

Lucy slid a look at her sister. How much *did* Elise know? Was she at all aware of Carlo's feelings for her? Lucy didn't think so. Even though, when Elsie had married her husband, John, six years before, it had been clear to anyone paying close attention that Carlo had lost the girl of his dreams.

Lucy had noticed because he'd been the man of hers, but she doubted that Carlo had ever deliberately shared with others how being best man at Elise's wedding had broken his heart. Lucy might have doubted it herself, except on the big day, wearing her own bridesmaid's tulle, she'd overheard Carlo's sister guess aloud his bitter secret. Lucy's own heart had fractured as he'd reluctantly confirmed the truth. The woman of his dreams was walking down the aisle. Away from him.

But it hadn't changed the way she felt about him, ever. Just as his stiff expression when she'd mentioned her sister made it clear his feelings for Elise were rock solid.

It was why Lucy hadn't made up her mind about what to do tonight. Should she really go? There was still time to claim a migraine or call in an excuse of stomach cramps.

Still uncertain, she reached for a hanger draped with a stretchy garment in sunset colors and sprinkled with sequins. "What do you think about this?" she asked, holding the various straps and scraps of fabric against her terry-cloth robe.

Elise's laugh burst out.

"What?"

Her sister couldn't seem to stop grinning. "Oh, I think you're going to be good for our Carlo."

Her Carlo, Lucy corrected. "I don't understand."

"Let's put it this way. Getting out of police work and into his own successful business didn't lighten up the man."

"Losing a partner to a bullet might account for that," Lucy defended, frowning at her sister. "Patrick McMillan was like a second father to Carlo."

Elise sighed. "It wasn't a criticism."

Crossing to the bed, Lucy tossed the dress down and then grabbed a bottle of lotion from the dresser and started to smooth the cream over her legs. "What did you mean by it, then?"

"You've seen how he's changed over the years," her sister said. "He used to smile more. Heck, he used to laugh. But now he ducks from most of the invitations our group of friends sends out, and when he does say yes, he broods in a corner or brings a date who does all his talking for him."

Like that too-pretty Tamara? Though apparently she was yesterday's news.

"I don't think he knows how to have fun anymore." Elise nodded toward the spangled dress stretched across the bedspread. "Maybe you could make that part of your job description."

Lucy's palm stopped halfway up her shin. "Aren't you afraid I'd botch that up just like I've botched up every other job I've had since graduation?" She knew that's what they all thought, even though leaving her positions in the accounting departments of the law firm, the school district and the insurance company had been completely voluntary. It wasn't that she hadn't done good work…it was that she hadn't *enjoyed* it.

Elise rolled her eyes. "You've been listening to our brothers too much."

"*And* Dad. And then there's Mom, who just keeps giving me these worried glances." Elise wasn't so innocent, either. All of them couldn't fathom why Lucy had yet to find the right job.

"Remember," her sister said, "you're the baby of the family."

"But for pity's sake, I'm not a baby anymore!"

Elise nodded, then leaned over to pluck the almost-nothing dress from off its place on the mattress. "I'm getting that. But maybe it's time you made it clear to everyone else."

Oh, great, Lucy thought. Just another item to put on her list. Don't screw up the temp job, do get over Carlo, do make clear to the public-at-large that Lucy Sutton was no longer in pigtails and braces.

On that last thought, Carlo invaded her mind again.

I see that you're all grown-up.

A woman.

For a moment she'd actually believed he *did* see that. That he saw *her.* But then she'd mentioned Elise's name and he'd gone distant and cool. No more masculine gleam in his eyes and no more half smile on his mouth. As usual, for Carlo, it was always Elise.

So why should she go through with this "date" tonight? She could comfortably stay home and still torture herself with that particular piece of knowledge.

But no! She capped the lotion with a vehement snap. Elise was right. Lucy should be out there proving she was no longer the Suttons' silly youngest sibling. Tonight didn't have to be about Carlo. Or about Carlo and Elise. Or about Carlo, and never Lucy.

Tonight could be about Lucy alone. If she focused on herself, maybe she could move into the future, leaving him the lone soul left wallowing in what-couldn't-be. Tonight, she should, no, she *would* go to the party as a single, sophisticated woman instead of a goosey love-struck girl.

Her older sister wandered off, leaving Lucy alone to finish prepping for the evening. After putting on make-up and smoothing her hair into straight strands with the flat iron, she wiggled into the stretchy dress she'd selected, adjusting the straps over her braless breasts and criss-crossing them on her bare back in order to tie the ends at her waist. Then she inspected herself in the mirror.

Okay. This was no baby-sister kind of dress. She'd purchased it at a boutique in Phoenix, at a supersale that even then cleaned out her clothing budget. The colors—ranging from palest yellow to the most passionate pink—mimicked a Southwest sunset and brightened her blond hair and fair skin. She paired it with high-heeled pink sandals and a raspberry lip gloss guaranteed to last all night long.

Through kisses and anything else, the product's sexy ad promised.

She didn't let her mind go *there,* though then it did, even without her permission. But why not? Maybe she would meet an attractive man at the party. Maybe he would kiss her.

It could happen.

She heard the doorbell ring, followed by the distant murmur of voices. Her brother-in-law, John's, the deeper rumble of Carlo's.

Her little shiver was merely because the night was turning cooler, of course.

So stifling any second thoughts, she grabbed a gauzy wrap and her evening purse, then headed out of the bedroom and down the hallway. A single, sophisticated woman on the way to a party.

Despite herself, her forward motion stopped just short of the living room. From her place in the shadows, she took in the tableau in front of her.

Her sister and brother-in-law were seated on the

couch, Lucy's "date" standing before them. Carlo was dressed in ash-gray slacks and a matching ash-gray silky-looking T-shirt, topped by a black linen sports jacket. He looked relaxed and, well, rich, the shine of his loafers mimicking the gleam of his dark hair. His mouth curved in polite amusement as John related something funny about work. After a moment, Carlo's eyes flickered away from his friend's face to light on Lucy's sister's classic features.

It seemed to her that his smile faded and his eyes turned empty.

Perhaps she made some movement then, giving herself away, because Carlo's gaze suddenly jumped to where Lucy was lurking. Hoping to cover for her staring, she immediately stepped into the living room, her shoulders back, her hips swaying. A sophisticated, single woman on her way to a party.

A sophisticated single woman who watched Carlo's carefully blank expression turn to one of blatant disapproval.

Her first-day nerves returned with a vengeance. Hives felt as if they were rising all over her skin. She would have turned and run, but her sophisticated, single-girl high heels allowed for no fast getaways.

Carlo Milano didn't like parties in general. He didn't like the one he was headed to tonight in particular. In particular, because he was accompanied by five feet and a hundred pounds of potential danger. Five feet and a hundred pounds of potential danger wearing high heels and a flaming-hot dress.

Closing his eyes as he shut the passenger door on her and the view of her bare, slender legs, he allowed himself a groan. If only he hadn't broken things off with Tamara, she would be his date tonight.

Tamara and her palpable hopes for a happily-ever-after life story, with him starring as the male lead.

It was why he'd been forced to end what had been pleasantly pleasant enough. When she'd started making noises about shared vacations and opportunities to meet her parents, he'd felt honor-bound to halt her building expectations. He just didn't think that type of happy ending was written into the Carlo Milano movie script.

Not that he didn't believe in happy endings. He'd seen his sister and many of his friends successfully couple up. Not for a minute did he doubt their commitments to their lovers. He went to each wedding wishing them all the best.

But at one wedding… At one wedding he'd started letting go of the notion of a lifelong romantic partnership for himself.

Then, when he'd lost his police partner to an unfair and untimely murder…he'd been certain he was destined to do the life thing solo.

Not to mention it just seemed simpler that way.

"La Jolla isn't in this direction," piped up the young beauty beside him. "I thought you said the party was in La Jolla."

He kept his focus out the windshield instead of glancing again at the blonde wrapped in salsa that was little Lucy Sutton all grown-up. Curse whatever combination of curiosity and kindness had prompted him to ask her out in the first place.

Kindness.

Right. The truth was, the water-cooler incident in the break room had snapped something inside of him. One moment he'd been remembering her as a bubblegum-popping tweenie, the next he was seeing her as a woman. Desirable. Beddable.

Though not available, of course. Not available to him, anyway. There were several reasons that made that a fact: she was an old family friend and almost like a little sister to him; her brothers were among his best friends and would beat him to a pulp if he and Lucy hooked up and he ended up hurting her; and he'd never forgive himself if—when—that very likelihood came to pass.

Still, aware of all that, he'd opened his big mouth and extended the invitation.

So here he was with Lucy. Desirable. Beddable.

Pure trouble.

His years as a street cop, then as a detective, then as a security expert had finely honed his instincts, and his instincts said she was mischief in the making. Lucy Sutton wearing that dress and looking like that in it was going to be up to her curvy hips in trouble tonight if he didn't stay on the ball.

"Carlo?"

He sighed. "We're making a stop before the party." Thank God. Anything to minimize the amount of time he'd have to be on guard-dog patrol. "You wouldn't by any chance dislike loud music and large crowds?"

He caught her grin out of the corner of his eye. "I *love* loud music and large crowds."

"Figures," he grumbled.

She laughed. "Why are we going, then, if you dislike the party scene so much?"

"You know. It's a work obligation." His calendar bulged with them. In a convention town that was also home to major league sports teams and that hosted big-name golf tournaments, as well as big-star rock concerts, McMillan & Milano's services were in constant demand. "The company's in charge of security for the Street Beat festival three weeks from now and I've got to put in an appearance and do the good ol' grip-and-grin for at least a few minutes."

Fewer than few, if he could get away with it. If Lucy Sutton had rattled him, not only a family friend but a man known as Mr. Keep-It-Light-and-Loose, what effect might she have on males who were actively prowling?

He shook his head. She was heading for trouble, all right.

Flipping his car's signal indicator, he turned right into the driveway of a well-maintained two-story, his gaze noting that the landscaping crew was keeping the hedges manicured and the lawns fertilized per his orders. The porch light added a cheery brightness to the entry, complete with a wreath of dried fall foliage on the front door.

"Come in with me," he suggested to Lucy. "You've met Germaine McMillan before, haven't you? I said I'd stop by and take care of a minor repair for her."

Again, he kept his eyes off Lucy's legs as she exited the car. But he couldn't keep her light scent away from his nose as they waited for Germaine to answer the ringing doorbell. The fragrance had caught his attention in the break room at the office, too, and remembering that brought back that quick flash he'd had of her plump, pretty breasts rising from the white lace cups of her bra.

To distract himself from the memory, he ran his hand over the molding around the doorjamb. Good. The paint was tight.

For some damn reason, so the hell were the muscles south of his waistline.

He could have kissed Germaine for choosing that instant to open the door. Actually, he did kiss her, an obligatory peck on her soft cheek that dimpled as he moved away and brought his companion forward.

"Do you remember Lucy Sutton?" he asked his partner's widow. "I'm sure you've met her before, as well as various other members of the Sutton family over the years."

"Of course!" Germaine appeared delighted by the company, which was part of the reason why he'd scheduled the stop. Like the landscaping, he could have hired out the minor repair. But without children or grandchildren of her own, Carlo knew the older woman enjoyed his visits. Just as he'd felt obligated to keep Patrick McMillan's name as part of the security firm the two of them had dreamed up before Pat's death, Carlo felt obligated to be the family Germaine didn't have. "Can I get you two some coffee and dessert?" she asked.

They followed her into the immaculate living room, where fresh vacuum trails showed clearly on the cream carpet. "Nothing for me, thanks," Lucy replied. "We're on our way to a party."

Germaine sat down on the floral couch and Lucy followed suit. "I shouldn't be keeping the pair of you, then."

Carlo waved his hand. "There's no rush. We have plenty of time. The party's bound to be boring, anyway."

And Lucy would be a whole lot easier to watch over among the flower fields that were Germaine's upholstered furniture than she would be at a party filled with rock musicians, businessmen and media types.

"Oh, you," Germaine scolded. "A man your age should enjoy a little nightlife."

Lucy leaned toward her. "We're not even there yet and he's already grumping about the music being too loud. Who knew what a fuddy-duddy he'd turn out to be?"

"Fuddy-duddy?" He frowned at her. *Fuddy-duddy?* For some reason the teasing jab ignited his usually cool temper. "Is that what you think? But coming from someone dressed in nothing more than a scanty pair of handkerchiefs, I'll take that as a compliment."

Lucy's spine straightened. She looked a little bit insulted, too. "Handkerchiefs? I'll have you know this dress is—"

"Outrageous?" *Fuddy-duddy.* He couldn't get the insult out of his mind. "An invitation to pneumonia?"

Her berry-colored mouth fell open and her blue, blue eyes narrowed. "You're—"

"Children, children," Germaine interrupted, her voice verging on laughter. "Maybe we should change the subject."

"You're right." Annoyed by his own out-of-character

reaction to Lucy's silly jibes, Carlo shoved his hands in his pockets. "I'll do better than that and in fact change the washers of the dripping faucet like I said I would."

Germaine started to rise, but he shook his head. "I know where I'm going and I know where you keep Pat's tools."

He couldn't exit the living room fast enough. If he didn't already know that Lucy had potential to be a snag in the smooth path of his planned evening, that last exchange would have been proof positive. How the hell had she gotten under his skin so fast?

Fuddy-duddy. Grumping. Good God, he didn't grump. How ridiculous.

But damn, if the descriptions hadn't rankled.

Passing the hall portrait of his late partner on the way to the dripping bathroom faucet, Carlo felt his mood dip even lower. As he tinkered, he thought of Pat's stocky frame and square, capable hands. The man should be here, Carlo thought on a sudden stab of sadness. Pat should be here, working out of his own red toolbox while looking forward to an evening of yet another TV documentary on military history, as well as a slice of his wife's famous mocha cheesecake.

Instead, Carlo's partner was gone.

Gone forever.

Upon completion of the repair, his footsteps were as heavy as his frame of mind as he returned to the living room. Hesitating at the archway, he listened to Germaine's amused voice.

"Then he turned the corner as fast as his old legs could go, wheezing, he said, sure that he'd lost the suspect, only to find the teenager caught on a cyclone fence, hanging upside down by his own oversize trousers."

Carlo remembered the moment as if it were yesterday and he couldn't resist adding to the story. "His own oversize trousers that had fallen down to his ankles, leaving his, uh, assets flapping in the breeze." Coming farther into the room, he couldn't help but grin at the memory. "Pat picked up the fancy cell phone that had fallen out of the boy's pocket and took a picture for posterity, while the dumb kid yammered on and on about police brutality."

He laughed. "Pat told him the only brutal thing about the event was his having to be subjected to a view of the kid's skinny butt." Laughing again, he recalled the expression of insulted outrage on the perp's upside-down face.

"Oh, Carlo."

The odd note in Germaine's voice zeroed his gaze in on her. "What?"

She smiled. "It's good to hear you laugh. It's good that we can remember my Pat with lightness in our hearts. He'd want that."

Carlo felt the smile he was wearing die as yet another pang of sadness sliced through him. All that Pat had wanted was to grow old with his beloved wife. Just a few relaxed and peaceful years of happily-ever-after.

He turned away, embarrassed by his sudden grief and just as determined to hide it. His hand speared through his hair and he cleared his throat. "Anything else I can do for you, Germaine?" His voice still sounded thick.

"No, but, Carlo…" Germaine's own suddenly teary voice filled with a sympathy he couldn't handle, yet couldn't run away from, either. Without looking at her, he sensed her rising and he steeled himself, desperate not to be weakened by any more emotion.

But then Lucy was there first, her hand looping around his arm. "Well, then I think we should be going, Germaine. I have to get the fuddy-duddy to the party before he turns into a pumpkin."

A new jolt of annoyance overrode his other feelings. *Fuddy-duddy* again! *Pumpkin*. He shook his head, frowning down into her bright face and naughty smile.

"Brat," he murmured. Okay, beautiful, but a brat all the same.

Germaine brightened. "Yes, yes. You must go on to your evening out."

Lucy's answer was to tug him toward the door. "Did you hear that, Carlo? Let's get a move on or next thing I know you'll be too busy filling out your AARP membership forms to find your way to a party."

Half-amused by her burst of energy and half-bemused by her second round of insults, he allowed her to pull him through the front door and toward his car. Even without a rock band, she was already dancing along the pavement and chattering away about the stars, the clear sky, how happy she was to be back in San Diego, which always held a hint of ocean in the night air.

When he pulled out of the driveway, he realized he was smiling again. Relaxed. She took a breath and he took advantage of the brief moment of quiet. "Lucy, I'm…"

"Feeling better?"

His head jerked her way. Her gaze was on him, her eyes big. Empathetic.

She knew.

She'd known he was close to losing it back there in Germaine's living room.

It was as embarrassing as hell to realize, but now it was clear that Lucy had intentionally come to his rescue. By stepping in with her sassy attitude and smart remarks, Lucy had given him the time and the distraction necessary to compose himself. Germaine hadn't needed him dumping his sorrow on top of her own.

Lucy had made sure he didn't.

"Lucy…" He was at a loss for words, still embarrassed that she'd read him so easily. Swallowing, he tried again. "You…"

She sent him that bright brat smile and fiddled with the hem of her too-short dress. "Look great in a pair of handkerchiefs, right?"

His gaze fell to her half-naked legs, then jumped back to the impish curve of her bright berry mouth. His blood rushed south and he felt that recognizable tightness at his groin. Of course, it couldn't be because of Lucy and how good she smelled and how delectable she looked in that dress. She was an old family friend, so it wasn't—

Oh, fine. What the hell. Why deny it? He was a man, with all the normal male responses. The truth was, old family friend or not, Lucy Sutton turned him on.

The admission sent his cop instincts hog wild again. This time they had another loud-and-clear message. *Be careful,* they told him. *Be very careful.*

She was still the little sister of some of his best friends, Elise and the sisters' brothers, Jason and Sam.

The Suttons and the Milanos had been connected for years and would continue to be connected for years to come.

So don't risk introducing awkwardness into the mix.

So don't risk getting too close to a woman who'd already shown herself adept at understanding his moods.

He took another breath of her sweet, feminine perfume. *Yeah, Milano, don't risk getting too close.* Because of the two people sitting in the butter leather seats of his Lexus, he had the sudden premonition that the one most likely to get into trouble tonight was him.

Chapter Three

Carlo Milano was wrong about a lot of things, Lucy decided, as they entered the Street Beat party. One, the music *wasn't* too loud, and two, judging by what other women were wearing who were in attendance, there was nothing unusual about her cocktail attire.

"Fuddy-duddy," she muttered to herself.

He leaned closer. "What?"

She glanced up. Okay, he didn't look like a fuddy-duddy, not with those incredible dark lashes surrounding his incredible dark eyes, and not with the way his wide shoulders filled out his casual linen jacket. And she wasn't the only one to have noticed his dearth of duddiness, either. She'd seen it in the eyes of other women they'd passed, and now, good Lord, now there was a tall, statuesque brunette wearing a slinky animal print sliding out of the crowd to close in on them like a leopard scenting a tasty meal.

The feline woman was still two dozen feet away when she called out the name of her prey. "Carlo!"

Lucy couldn't help it, she stepped closer to him. Her hip brushed his groin, and she all at once recalled her plan for the evening. *Not* sticking close to Carlo. *Not* fostering dreams that couldn't be.

Remember? She was a single, sophisticated woman at a party. A single, sophisticated woman who should be looking for other single sophisticates, but of the masculine variety. Clearing her throat, she ignored the approaching woman and started edging away from Carlo's body. "I think I'll go—"

"Stay," he said against her ear. It felt more like a kiss than a command and she froze, making it easy for him to hook two fingers into the waistline at the back of her dress. She felt his knuckles press against her naked skin.

"Carlo—"

"I'll give you a raise if you'll just play along."

There wasn't any more time to protest. The brunette appeared before them on a waft of Chanel No. 5. "Mr. Milano," she said in a scolding voice. "This is beyond fashionably late."

Then the woman moved in for the kill—uh, greeting—and Lucy tried to edge away again. Carlo's fingers curled tighter on her dress, though, plastering her as snugly against him as a "Hi, My Name Is" sticker.

The action forced the other woman to settle for an air kiss in the vicinity of his chin. Then she gave Lucy a cursory glance. "I'm Claudia Cox," she said, holding out her hand even as her gaze returned to Carlo. "So... Who's your little friend?"

Lucy gritted her teeth and gave a little handshake as Carlo answered. "This is Lucy Sutton. She's just back in town from Phoenix."

Claudia flicked another glance in her direction. "Really? I thought you were seeing Tamara."

His hand slipped out of Lucy's dress to slide around her waist and then press possessively against her hip bone. She tried to look as if her knees were melting—for Claudia's benefit—without standing as if her knees *were* really melting—for Carlo's.

"I'm with Lucy now." He pressed a kiss to the top of her head and her scalp prickled from crown to nape.

"Lucky Lucy," Claudia commented, wearing a thin smile.

Lucy thought it was time to chime in and prove to them all she still had a voice. "That's just what I say to myself every time I hear this man say my name. It's nice to meet you, Claudia." Then she entwined her fingers with those of Carlo's that were wrapped at her hip and tried to subtly peel them off before her dress started to smolder.

His touch made her just that hot.

Carlo allowed their joined hands to fall to her side, but stroked hers with a caressing thumb when Claudia's gaze dropped to their fingers.

"We need to set up a meeting," the other woman told Carlo, her voice a bit sharp, "since it doesn't look as if you're prepared to talk business tonight."

Behind her, Lucy felt Carlo straighten. His thumb stopped its distracting movement. "What's up, Claudia?"

The other woman looked at Lucy. "Do you mind…?"

"Oh, no," she said, taking the hint. "I'll just go over to the bar and leave you two alone—"

"Sweetheart, you know I don't like you out of my sight." Carlo's fingers squeezed hers. Tight.

Lucy swallowed her wince. "Isn't he cute?" she said to Claudia, then looked up at her date. "Darling, I won't go far."

"Baby, I don't think so." His hand gave hers another warning squeeze. "Stay with me."

Baby? That's what she was supposed to be proving she *wasn't* tonight. And she knew he was a boy big enough to handle leopard lady and whatever the heck she wanted to discuss in private.

Lucy beamed Carlo a sickly smile. "Handsome, Claudia wants to talk about business, and you know how little me gets so sleepy when talk turns to numbers and such."

Of course, that was uncomfortably close to the truth. And uncomfortably terrible for someone who'd graduated with honors and an accounting degree to admit.

Claudia shook her head, apparently impatient with them both. "It's not about numbers. I only wanted to let you know that I've okayed a parents group from a local high school to help out with the security."

"Street Beat security?" He sent Lucy a glance, then went on to explain, "Claudia's the festival promoter."

"For the past five years," the older woman added before turning her attention to Carlo again. "The parents are going to use their pay as a fund-raiser for their kids' senior prom. The fairgrounds did something similar last summer. It will be good PR for us."

He frowned. "But parents? I don't know, Claudia. I'll want to talk to the fair security people, and even if they think it went well, I'm not sure—"

"Oh, you should at least consider it," Lucy interjected. "I was part of a community group that raised money in Phoenix last year during the hot air balloon festival weekend. We helped out with security and parking. It worked out great for everyone concerned."

"Yeah?" Carlo lifted an eyebrow.

Even Claudia was looking at Lucy with more interest. "Yes," she confirmed. "We had kids involved, too, because they're always looking for ways to beef up their college applications with community service. If they were over sixteen and accompanied by a parent, they were welcome, too."

"Carlo," Claudia said, looking less leopardlike and more thoughtful. "That sounds even better to me. I think it could increase future ticket sales if more teenagers are exposed to the festival."

"I see your point, but—"

"It's not supplanting your security plans," Claudia insisted. "It's supporting them. The volunteers can do simple things like move barriers and keep order in the food lines."

Carlo switched his gaze to Lucy. "How much do you know about how it worked in Phoenix?"

She shrugged. "It was my baby. I pulled the volunteers together, I worked with the regular balloonfest security people, I spent the weekend slathered in sunscreen and passing out water bottles. It's like Claudia said, we were essentially gofers for the professional security team and we made good money for a local women's shelter."

"Sounds like you made it a success."

"It didn't take a brain trust, just attention to detail and an ability to organize people. I can give you the phone number of a guy in Phoenix—"

"Don't bother," he said. "Any calls that need to be made you can do yourself. This endeavor in San Diego will be your baby, too."

She stared at him. "My baby?"

"Your project. You work for McMillan & Milano."

"Well, yes." And apparently in his rush to deflect predator Claudia's interest he hadn't concerned himself about what the other woman might think about his mixing business with pleasure inside his own office.

"So I'm putting you in charge of the high school volunteers at the Street Beat festival."

"I work for McMillan & Milano answering your phone and bringing you your mail," she protested.

Carlo waved it away. "Because you agreed to help out with that job as a favor, not because it's the position you're suited for. You're the one with experience managing a volunteer activity like this. And even though you say it doesn't take a brain trust, I happen to know you have a sharp mind, as well as a college degree your parents are very proud of. So, I've decided. It's your project, Lucy."

It's my project. Just something else to potentially screw up in the next three weeks because, lucky for her, the music event was scheduled at the end of her time with Carlo's company. Was it now that she told him? Was it now she admitted that in the years since graduation she'd yet to find a position she *was* suited for? Surely, like the Suttons, he'd see it as a major flaw in her character that not one of her accounting jobs had floated her boat. Unlike her forge-straight-ahead family, she'd yet to find her path to success. She opened her mouth.

Claudia beat her to the punch. "Carlo…" The other woman's lips moved into a moue of distress and she lowered her voice as if she considered Lucy deaf, as well as dumb. "Do you really think your little phone answerer is the right person for the job?"

Little.

Little phone answerer.

Lucy's spine snapped straight as she heard in those words and that voice echoes of other words, other voices.

Little Lucy.

Lucy Goosey.

Lucy won't do it right this time, either.

Carlo lifted one dark brow. "Lucy?"

She swallowed. No way could she back down now, not in front of Claudia of the leopard dress and superior attitude, not in front of Carlo, who would likely pass along her balking to her sister and brothers, not in front of *herself* who had so many things to prove.

And now add one more.

"Don't worry, Claudia," she said. "His little phone answerer will be just fine."

Oh, how she wished she'd stuck to her plan and unstuck herself from Carlo. It was too late, though. There was nothing else to do but accept, and then succeed at this Street Beat assignment. She pushed away her panic at the thought, even though in the past three years she hadn't truly felt successful at much besides finding another job after leaving the previous one behind.

Somehow, Lucy had gotten away from him. The longer Carlo didn't see her among the crowd at the Street Beat party, the more anxious he was to get his hands on her—uh, correct that. The more anxious he was to get a bead on where she was. *Hands* off, *Milano*. It was the cop inside him talking again, and his good sense, too. *Hands off.*

Shoving them inside his pockets, he scanned the room, his gaze searching the people either standing in small groups or gyrating to the rock music on the small dance floor. Where the hell was she?

Keeping an eye on her was his obligation, wasn't it? Because he'd invited her tonight, because he was her boss, and most of all, because he'd known her and her family since Lucy still had training wheels on her bicycle.

Before adulthood had given her hips and smooth, curvy legs and that seductive smile that had him heading toward her for the intercept. Blame it on his cop intuition again.

Then Carlo's gaze narrowed and a skitter of irritation shot up his spine. No wonder he was on edge. Take a look at her dance partner! Long shaggy hair, pierced eyebrow, motorcycle boots. He picked up his pace.

Consequently, he was nearby when a wild spin took her into his territory. Carlo caught her in his arms.

Her face flushed, she looked up at him. "Oh."

His hands slid from her shoulders to her hips. He'd held that sweet curve of hers before—and had had trouble keeping his mind focused on Claudia and business.

He squeezed. There was the smallest give to her flesh and his fingers sank into it as he took a deep breath of her tempting, female scent. "You ran away from me," he said.

"Ran away? Carlo, I didn't know you cared," she teased. Her lashes dropped, and she gave him another one of those flirtatious, womanly glances.

Just like that, his male instincts overrode his inner cop talk, causing his palms to slide up her curves to her waist as he drew her nearer. "Lucy…"

Lucy!

His hands dropped. This was *Lucy,* and she was here as his family friend, his temporary employee, as someone he should be looking after, not looking to touch.

She used her new freedom to sketch him a wave before twirling back onto the dance floor and into the proximity of the grinning possible felon, who then grabbed her by the hand. Irritation spiking again, Carlo elbowed the man standing beside him.

"Excuse me. Do you know that guy over there?"

"Huh?"

"The one with the red lightning bolt crawling up his skinny right arm." The dude was dressed in leather pants, of all things, and a muscle shirt that clung to his scrawny chest.

"That's Wrench."

Good God. He was named after a tool. "Wrench who?"

"Just Wrench. He's the lead singer of Silver Bucket."

Silver Bucket. Before she'd disappeared on him, he'd listened to Lucy discuss with Claudia the musical lineup for the Street Beat festival. That had gotten the older woman's attention away from Carlo and he'd been glad. After a few minutes it was clear Lucy knew her music, impressing Claudia and amusing Carlo.

Until now. She'd professed a deep love for the music of Silver Bucket and here she was boogeying down with Silver Bucket's lead singer. Wrench.

For God's sake, that wasn't funny.

Frowning, he settled back on his heels to watch what happened next. The protective stance and attitude was just what he needed, he decided, to put away those dangerous and recurring moments he'd spent seeing Lucy as a woman.

Of course, she wasn't a little girl any longer, either. No one seeing her in that dress—two hankies, no matter how she denied it—could see her as anything less than an attractive, desirable, adult female.

The lead singer had noticed, that's for sure.

"Wrench," Carlo muttered.

Though loud enough, apparently, for the man standing next to him to hear. He cocked a brow in Carlo's direction. "You do know Silver Bucket, right?"

"Uh…" Great, he was going to be forced to admit that he *was* a fuddy-duddy.

The other man took pity on him. "They're the ones

known for their shock-and-awe pyrotechnics show during their signature song, 'Mosh Pit.' It always works the crowd into a frenzy."

Shock-and-awe pyrotechnics. "Mosh Pit."

Frenzy.

Tension grabbed the back of Carlo's neck and he took his eyes off Lucy to seek out Claudia. There wasn't going to be any pyrotechnics, mosh pits or, for that matter, frenzies at the upcoming festival. Not when he was head of security.

With a glimpse of Claudia near the bar and thwarting possible future catastrophe at the forefront of his mind, he cast a last glance at Lucy and then set his jaw and left her unguarded. Surely she wouldn't go far.

Ten minutes later, Claudia's promises had appeased his uneasiness. Five minutes later, it was back again. Lucy was nowhere to be found. And neither was Wrench.

Her voice echoed in his head. *"I just adore that band."*

Carlo's mind abandoned common sense and leaped to a worst-case scenario. If she eloped with Wrench, her family would never forgive him. *He* would never forgive himself.

Lucy was like a...a...almost like a sister to him.

Sister. Right.

Pulse pumping, he strode toward the dessert buffet and the exit doors just beyond. A guy like Wrench would have a limo, wouldn't he? Maybe he and Lucy were in it right now, speeding toward Vegas, and the tool was popping champagne and eyeing her spectacular legs as she stretched out on black leather. Hell.

"Wearing a face like that, you could scare people."

At the sound of Lucy's voice, Carlo spun. Damn it! Preoccupied by the vision in his mind, he'd hurried right past her. She stood on the far side of the dessert tables, half-hidden by a fountain bubbling waterfalls of white chocolate.

"There you are," he said.

Her eyes widened. "Were you looking for me?"

It took concentration, but he managed to relax his shoulders. He hadn't lived in this world for thirty-four years without learning a thing or two. Telling Lucy he'd been looking *out* for her might give a rise to her hackles.

"It's getting late," he said instead. "I was after some dessert before I rounded you up in order to leave." To put truth to his words, he grabbed a plate and started scooping up random items.

She waited for him to finish, then together they wandered out onto a small terrace. It was almost empty of people, but a few small waist-high tables were set up under portable heaters.

He took a breath of the fresh air, then looked over at her. "Having fun?"

She held a white-chocolate-covered strawberry to her parted lips. "Mmm." Nodding, she took a bite out of the juicy thing.

He should look away.

He couldn't look away.

Damn, but there went his common sense again, evaporating under the radiant warmth of the patio heaters—not to mention the radiant warmth that was his libido catching fire.

A drip of pink-tinged juice oozed at the corner of her mouth and she tongued it off. Carlo cleared his throat, tore his gaze away, then couldn't stop it from jerking back.

"There," he muttered, gesturing at her with his fork.

Her eyebrows came together. "There? There where? There what?" She whipped her head around in confusion.

"There on your mouth." Carlo was forced to step closer. "Some of that white chocolate." A dab perched on the rosy pillow of her bottom lip.

Her tongue's next search-and-destroy mission completely missed the spot.

He couldn't stand to watch her send it out again and he couldn't look at the creamy dot for one more second. "Let me," he said impatiently. The edge of his thumb touched down.

And seemed to stick to her bottom lip as if the sugary stuff was superglue.

Her gaze jolted to his. Her breath burned his hand.

Time froze.

Carlo remembered he was a family friend. A former cop who could smell trouble from two blocks away. A man who thought of himself as Mr. Keep-It-Light.

But his blood was hot and heavy, chugging slowly through his veins. Lucy's big blues were looking at him as if she sensed the same thing he did. Attraction in the air. Just like that moment two years ago, a moment he'd thought he'd banished from his memory forever.

Because this was attraction he had no business feeling, not for someone so young, so fresh, so flat-out deserving of all the happily-ever-afters a man like him could never promise. That a man like him didn't want to promise because he couldn't take a chance on all the painful ways ever-after could end instead.

Still, as he stroked his thumb free of her mouth, he couldn't stop himself from thinking he was freeing it for something else....

He leaned closer.

Lucy shifted left, her eyes widening. "Oh! Thanks." She used a little square of napkin to scrub his touch away. "I'm not usually so...so..."

Cowardly? Carlo thought. No, no. He meant smart. Smarter, for sure, than him, because a second ago he'd been close to overriding his brain. His gray matter knew it was crazy to play around with Lucy, even though parts farther south were still registering the fact they considered the idea had some merit.

"So what's with you and Claudia, anyway?" Lucy asked with a shiny smile.

He groaned. "Nothing, and that's just the way I like it."

She nodded. "I figured as much when I was pressed into playing your latest girlfriend."

He looked over his shoulder. "Keep it down, okay? Claudia gets wind it was a ruse and I'm toast."

"Why don't you just tell her you're not interested?"

"Does she strike you as a woman who takes no for an answer? I think the challenge would only cause her to slow long enough to sharpen her claws for the final takedown."

Lucy laughed. "Okay, I clued in on the she-cat resemblance myself, but I have to say that by the time I finished talking to her about Street Beat, I found myself actually liking her."

"She's a hell of a businesswoman, but just not the woman I want in my bed."

At that last phrase, the smile on Lucy's face slid away. Her eyes went wide once more.

And again, the hands of his watch seemed to stop.

His comment begged the question—and all of a sudden it was sizzling in the air between them as if she'd spoken it aloud—who *was* the woman he wanted in his bed?

Lucy.

No matter how wrong the idea was, no matter how many reasons why not, it was suddenly there.

Lucy.

Damn that stinkin', inconvenient, completely unasked-for sexual chemistry.

Yet despite his condemnation he found himself leaning toward her again. Leaning toward her luscious berry lips.

Halfway there, she blinked, as if sensing danger. Her arm jerked up and she held her fork between them like a weapon. "You…" She swallowed hard, her fluster showing in her new flush. "You have something on your dessert plate I didn't get. That…that pie thing."

"Uh-huh." He didn't give that…that pie thing a glance. He was still preoccupied with the idea of Lucy in his bed—or at the very least of Lucy's kiss against his mouth.

No.

Lucy was a little sister to him…except she wasn't.

Lucy was just a kid…except she wasn't anymore. Lucy didn't want him to kiss her…except she was swaying toward him, and her gaze was fixed on his mouth as if she were willing it to come closer to hers.

He found himself moving nearer.

Was he really this weak? Apparently he was. Or the attraction was just that strong.

He couldn't look away from her berry lips and the wet tip of her tongue, which darted out to touch the top one. Now was the last chance to dredge up his common sense, to gather his brain cells together, to do something other than give in.

However, the whiz-bang-pow between them had a mind and will of its own and he found himself unable to alter the course. She swallowed again. "What, uh, what would it take for me to get a bite?"

His laugh was low. "I'm sure we can think of something."

She didn't move as he took the fork out of her unresisting hand and set it on the table. And she didn't blink as he drew her against him. She didn't make a sound as he finally succumbed to temptation and lowered his mouth to taste hers.

Chapter Four

At the last second, Carlo hesitated, his breath mingling with Lucy's. What the hell was he doing? He prided himself on his honesty and he honestly couldn't figure out what impulse was driving him. As that straightforward and truthful man he knew himself to be, he shouldn't start something that he was never, ever going to see through.

But it's just a kiss, the devil on his shoulder whispered. *You're not promising anything more.*

And Lucy was so much more. So much more than the girl who used to amuse him. Now she was a woman with glistening, berry-colored lips and breath that smelled faintly of chocolate.

He wanted just a sample. An experimental caress. A small, not-enough-to-startle-her taste.

And she looked ready to startle. She stood frozen

before him, her gaze somewhere south of his, and he cupped her face between his hands to guide her mouth to a better alignment with his own. When she didn't protest, when instead her feathery lashes drifted down, so did Carlo's mouth.

His lips brushed across hers. *Careful, man,* he reminded himself. He reversed directions for another light stroke.

She trembled. *God.* The vibration traveled through him like a jolt of pure energy. He fought against the possessive need to tighten his fingers on her warm skin. When he caressed her mouth again, she gave another shiver, and the honesty of her instant response pierced him once more. It was like holding a butterfly in the gentle cage of his hands.

More energy buzzed through his body, tightening his muscles, but he fought against the tension. Lucy tasted so sweet. Lucy was sweet, so he was determined not to come on too strong.

But he wasn't yet ready to end the experiment. Not quite yet. With his fingers still cupping her from jaw to cheekbones, he brushed over her mouth again, giving her another soft kiss. She shivered again, and he felt another energizing buzz.

Slow, deliberate, he pressed his mouth harder against hers and felt her lips part under the new pressure. Still gentle, still careful not to startle her, he slid his tongue inside to give the tip of hers a tender greeting.

At the warm, wet touch, she made a small sound in the back of her throat and...

She bit him.

A sharp, edges-of-the-teeth erotic nip on the very tongue that he'd been trying so hard to keep gentle and nonthreatening.

He jerked his head back just as all his muscles jerked in hot, sexual reaction.

She was staring up at him, narrow-eyed, with a glint of something—anger?—in her eyes and a flush on her cheekbones.

"I'm…" Carlo started. Sorry? Was she warning him off? But she hadn't moved away, and when he started to lift his hands, she reached up to hold his wrists. Her cheeks felt hot against his palms.

"Do you call that a kiss?" she demanded.

Her voice echoed in his head. *Do you call that a kiss?*

If he was honest—and hadn't he just been thinking of his pride in that?—the restrained caress hadn't been a Carlo Milano kind of kiss. Carlo Milano didn't like fragile women or tentative touches. He was a red-blooded Italian male, and the kind of kisses he liked to give out were designed for grown-up females. Grown-up females like…

Lucy.

Lucy was all grown up, with her berry-pink lips and that damn, tantalizing, two-hankie dress. All. Grown. Up.

She must have read his mind. "I don't want a fuddy-duddy kiss, either."

At the taunt, his fingers tightened on her face and he tilted her sassy mouth higher. Oh, yeah, she was devilish, no doubt about it. Her hands dropped their hold on his wrists and wrapped around his neck to draw him nearer.

"That's right," she whispered, pulling him close. "If you're going to do this, I insist you do it right."

It was all the permission he needed. His lips crashed into hers and they opened immediately for him. She made that sound in her throat again, but it was needy now, womanly, and he thrust his tongue into her mouth to taste her yearning.

Sweet. Hot. Sexy.

Their tongues tangled and he slid his hands from her face down her back to the flare of her hips. He scooped them up against his and then barely suppressed his own groan. She was such a warm, curvy armful. When she trembled, his own muscles shuddered in response.

Her hands tangled in the hair at the back of his neck, and the sensation burned a trail down his spine and then raced to his groin, pulling his skin—and everything else—taut. She had to feel him against her flat belly, but her only response was to slant her head and take the kiss deeper.

Deeper. He'd give his right hand to find himself as deep inside her as he could be. No, no, not his right hand. He needed that, he realized, as it slid between their bodies and then up the delicate ladder of her ribs.

He needed it for *this*.

Her spine bowed as his **hand** moved between their bodies then cupped her breast. Her hips pressed harder to his as his thumb brushed across the hard bud of her nipple.

The smoke of desire's fire obscured everything but touching more, having more, wanting more, more,

more. Behind a hazy screen was his good sense, his cop hunches, his sense of who he was.

There was only this: Lucy in his arms, Carlo alive for the first time in God knew how many years, every part of him tingling with a rush of blood he hadn't experienced in longer than he cared to remember.

Maybe it had never been this good.

Maybe he'd never been this alive.

He slid the hand at her hip lower, cupping the round cheek of her cute behind in one hand while the other continued to play with her breast.

This was heaven.

"Whoops." Stifled laughter broke through the fog in Carlo's head. He opened his eyes without breaking the kiss and saw the interrupting couple disappear back inside the ballroom. Reality crashed like an anvil in a Coyote and Roadrunner cartoon.

This was hell.

They were on a public patio at a public, *professional* event, and he'd been all but ready to go all the way with his paid employee.

He leaped away.

Cleared his throat.

Buttoned his jacket to hide his erection.

Picked up the tepid coffee sitting on the nearby table and downed it in one bitter swallow.

Then there was nothing else to do but look at Lucy.

She was looking right back at him.

"Well." He drew one hand down his face. "I... That..." Taking a breath, he tried thinking of what to say next. What the hell was *wrong* with him? He still couldn't think, not with the smell of Lucy's perfume on his hands and the taste of her still delicious on his tongue.

Clearheaded Carlo Milano, former cop Carlo Milano, successful businessman Carlo Milano, was knocked on his butt by one blue-eyed, blond, family friend.

Oh. That's what was wrong with all this! *Now* he remembered. Lucy Sutton was enmeshed in his life in ways that went beyond the reception area. Though she might be his employee only temporarily, she was forever a part of his life—at least through his friendship with her siblings and parents.

He couldn't just play with Lucy, and that's all that he had in him when it came to women. Fun and games.

"Well, I… Well, you…" He gave an inward groan at his bumbling ineptitude. *You kissed the woman, Milano. Now straighten out the mess you've made.*

He cleared his throat, adjusted his jacket, looked at her face, looked away. "You… I…"

"Am going to freeze my buns off if we don't get somewhere warmer soon," she said. "Me, I mean. I can't speak for you, but this dress doesn't cut it against the sudden cold." Then she looked away, as if embarrassed about mentioning the abrupt change in temperature—when they both knew the abrupt change in temperature was because they were no longer in each other's arms.

His thumb tingled at the memory of the small round button that had been her nipple.

Shoving his hand in his pocket, he took a bracing breath. "Let's get you inside, then."

"And maybe out to the car?" she suggested. "It's late and I have that mean boss who'll expect me to be on time tomorrow, I'm sure."

"Yeah." Carlo strode for the door that would take them to the ballroom and pulled it open for her. Then he held his breath as she passed so he could avoid her sweet, beguiling scent.

All the way to the car and on the road to her sister's he stewed about what to say about the kiss that should never have happened. As much as he wanted to beat himself up about it, it didn't make the memories of those minutes any less compelling. How the hell were they going to work together without him thinking of it every damn second? How was he going to explain to her and himself how he'd let that interlude get so out of hand?

"It was just a curiosity queller," he murmured, trying out the sound of it.

"What?"

Oh, damn, he'd been muttering louder than he thought.

But it was the only halfway decent excuse he could think of. "Curiosity. You know."

"Explain, please."

He pretended the road needed all his attention. "We had to get it out of the way, right?"

"The kiss."

"Yeah." He shrugged. "It was there, in the air, you know, and so it was best to get it out of the way. We can forget about it now."

"Forget about it."

The way she was repeating his words in that monotone was annoying. *She* was annoying, he decided. Actually, that was an honest assessment of the whole situation, if you asked him. That dress was annoying, the way her blond hair caught the glow of the streetlights was annoying, the damn position he was in, turned on by the woman who was going to be answering his phones, was *way* beyond annoying.

He pulled into the driveway at her sister and brother-in-law's house.

"Don't tell Elise about this," he heard himself grind out. Because, hell, if Lucy told her bigmouth big sister it would get back to their brothers, who would then turn on Carlo...and what would he do then?

"Tell Elise about what?" Lucy said, her voice without expression.

"About, uh..."

"Us?"

He sighed. "Yeah."

"Why would I do that? There's nothing between us to report, is there?"

She said it so coolly. So matter-of-factly. In just the way he wanted. In just the way he had hoped for.

"Right," he answered. "Nothing to report. All forgotten. Nothing between us at all."

He was still mumbling nonsense phrases as she climbed out of the car. He waited until she'd let herself into the house.

"Nothing between us at all," he repeated to the closing front door. Then he thumped his forehead against the steering wheel. *Bump bump bump.*

With each tap he acknowledged that the man who so prided himself on honesty was now lying through his teeth.

Lucy decided that forgetting about that kiss—okay, series of kisses, and, well, more—on the patio during the Street Beat party was doable, if she wasn't around Carlo. But of course she was around Carlo, her temporary boss, *all the time.*

Even now, when they were on their way to a meeting at concert promoter Claudia Cox's Del Mar offices in northern San Diego County to discuss the volunteer program Lucy had been assigned to oversee. She snuck a look in Carlo's direction, then quickly jerked her glance back to the window. Sometimes she'd find herself staring at his face and remembering the sure thrust of his tongue and the thrilling caress of his lean fingers at her breast.

Oh, great. She felt her face heating up and she squirmed on the leather seat.

"What's the matter?" he asked.

"Nothing." She'd be in hell before she gave away that she was any more affected by what had happened than Carlo "Kiss Me Then Forget Me" Milano. Still, she couldn't help herself from frowning at him. "I could handle this meeting by myself."

"I don't mind coming along."

Well, she minded. He'd given her the job and he should have left her alone to handle it. He probably regretted the assignment. He probably thought she was incompetent, which wouldn't surprise her since the rest of her family did, too.

She yanked on the hem of her suit skirt and ironed out imaginary wrinkles with the flat of her hand. Maybe that was why he'd backed away from her so quickly at the party the other night. He thought she was incompetent when it came to kissing, too.

Hah. She'd prove him wrong. She'd show him she could handle her Street Beat duties just fine.

And she was *never* going to kiss him again.

With those resolves in mind, she strode into the concert promoter's offices with her best all-business attitude, then halted in the reception area to stare around her as if she was a little kid.

While Carlo's company's offices were dominated by those picture-postcard views of the bay, this office was dominated by...colors. Sounds.

Each curved wall delineating the receptionist's space was painted a different shade: cinnamon, goldenrod, turquoise. There was an emerald-green sisal carpet covering most of the blond hardwood floor. The plush chairs were upholstered in fabric that was in a bright Mexican design. On each wall was a flat screen playing music videos, each one at a volume just loud enough to create a cacophony that had Carlo wincing.

Lucy could only think of the three places she used to work. By some coincidence, in each of them the walls had been painted the same pale cadaver-green of graph paper. By far the most colorful ornamentation in any of the places had to be the freebie calendars the insurance company's national office had distributed each holiday season. Yep, that eleven-by-eleven-inch photograph of the Citizen's Insurance float at the Rose Bowl Parade had provided a much-needed visual punch.

However, there were many, many more ocular knockouts at the concert promoter's office, only one of which was the receptionist. She wore chartreuse leggings under a floating skirt and a matching blouse, and when she looked up from the phones that were set on a clear Lucite desktop there was a tiny sapphire stud in her nose and the two piercings below her left eyebrow showed off matching jewelry.

"May I—" she started, but then Claudia strode around a corner.

Today, the older woman was dressed in another eye-catching outfit. No animal print this time, but a canary-yellow pants outfit accented with print scarf in Picasso colors.

Carlo pushed Lucy forward with a gentle hand at the small of her back. "You remember Lucy."

As they briefly shook hands, Claudia's eyes ran over her, making Lucy feel dowdy in her gray pinstripes, even though she knew her mother had spent a hefty chunk for it as her post-college graduation "interview" suit. Her palms dampened and she rubbed them together. Great, already her confidence was eroding.

As Claudia gestured them down a hallway painted in more vibrant shades, she slanted Lucy another glance. "Who did you last work for, a mortician?"

A startled laugh escaped Lucy's mouth and she tried hard to swallow it back down, even as she felt her cheeks burn. "As a matter of fact, my older brother once set me up with a job interview at a mortuary." The mortician, thank God, hadn't found her right for the job. "But most places dress a little more corporate than here."

Still, she was beginning to wonder if her family didn't have a point. Maybe Lucy wasn't right for anything.

It made her steps heavy as she followed Claudia's subtle wave of Chanel No. 5 down the hall. With Carlo at her back, Lucy took a quick peek into an office where a young man in dreadlocks was chattering away on a headset. In another, a woman in jeans and a baby tee was shaking her shoulders to something she was listening to through bagel-size headphones.

Claudia glanced over shoulder. "My brother wanted me to be his medical transcriptionist," she said. "And my first husband wanted me to be a double-D cup."

As Lucy digested these interesting tidbits, the older woman paused by an alcove that contained a small refrigerator, a coffeemaker and an espresso machine. "Luckily, the one who got their wish was me."

Without waiting for a response or even asking what they'd like, Claudia reached inside the fridge to hand over slender containers of bottled water. Then she continued heading down the hall.

Lucy slowed so that Carlo came up beside her. "What about her second husband?" she whispered to him.

"Don't ask," he whispered back.

"I heard that." In front of a closed door, Claudia stopped again. "It's no secret. My second husband had me arrested for picking up his dry cleaning and then holding it hostage after I kicked the SOB out."

"Oh." Lucy felt her eyes widen. She *shouldn't* have asked. So far Lucy and her dowdy suit were only racking up negative points. "I'm, uh, sorry."

"Don't be." Claudia's beringed right hand whisked the sentiment away. "Because then I took him *to* the cleaners in the divorce. Now I have all this."

And with that, she swung open the closed door to reveal a conference room decorated in plum tones that held a long table, plush chairs and a small group of middle-aged parent-types who looked a bit over-whelmed by their splashy surroundings. They rose to their feet, and from the way their gazes fixed on Claudia, it looked as if they'd heard every one of her words and weren't sure whether they should run screaming or just plain run.

As if seeking solace, their heads turned toward Carlo, but his dark looks and unsmiling cop face were better suited for intimidation. Their tension seemed to increase until their gazes shifted again and found Lucy.

She almost laughed. Lucy Goosey had never alarmed anyone. Without thinking, she moved forward with a big smile, hoping to put the parents at ease.

"Hi," she said, holding out her hand to each one. "I'm Lucy Sutton and I'm so glad we could meet. I'll be coor-dinating your volunteer efforts at the Street Beat festival."

The group arranged themselves around the confer-ence table. Claudia, naturally, took the head position, and the parents wore those nervous expressions again. Maybe the concert promoter sensed the situation, be-cause she quickly turned over the discussion to Carlo, who passed it off to his "assistant."

Lucy found all eyes on her once more. Her stomach swooped and her hands were unsteady as she opened the manila folder she'd brought with her. Fanning out the paperwork gave her time to gather her thoughts.

What am I doing?

Why am I in charge?

What if I fail...?

I'd hate to look like a fool in front of Carlo.

My family will never let me hear the end of it.

Lucy Goosey, silly all over again.

Carlo's voice suddenly pierced through her loud fears. "Lucy coordinated a similar effort at last year's hot air balloon festival in Phoenix," he said. "It was a great success according to Arthur McGrath, who coordinated the entire event."

Lucy's head lifted. It *had* been a great success. And when had Carlo spoken with Art? She glanced over at him.

He made a little go-ahead gesture with his chin. "A great success," he repeated.

Lucy cleared her throat, then smiled again at the volunteers. "I know we can make this occasion work just as well for all of us and Street Beat."

The older people smiled back. They took out pencils and paper and then looked even happier when Lucy provided sheets that listed what she'd already discussed with Carlo. Outlined were the details about scheduling, what volunteers should wear and a copy of the necessary permission slips they'd need for the teens. They set up an evening meeting at the McMillan & Milano offices, where they would go over with all the volunteers the layout of the festival and what exactly they would be doing.

Then it was over. Everyone was getting to their feet. "Excuse me," Carlo interjected into the casual wrap-up conversation. "Don't forget to hand these out, Lucy." He reached into his jacket pocket and passed over to her a stack of business cards.

She glanced down at them. Stopped. Stared. Lucy Sutton, they read. Security Technician.

Her forefinger ran over the embossed letters. Carlo had had business cards made up. For her.

For Lucy Goosey, his temporary employee.

But Lucy Goosey had handled this meeting with professional aplomb. The volunteers took the cards and tucked them away as they thanked Claudia for the opportunity and then Carlo and Lucy for their time, as well. Finally, the woman who appeared to be their leader held out her hand to Lucy. "We're *very* comfortable working with you."

All the way back to the San Diego security offices, Lucy made notes. Carlo mumbled something about her making herself carsick, but she ignored him to focus on the task at hand. By the time they made it back to McMillan & Milano, she was surprised to find it was way after 5:00 p.m. and that the lights were dimmed.

Carlo passed into his office and was checking his e-mails by only the glow of his monitor while she put her area to rights before leaving for the night. Her arms got hung up while she was trying to replace phone books on a high shelf, so she had to slip off her constricting suit jacket to reveal her white, lacy sleeveless blouse. "Let me know when you're ready to leave," he called through the open door. "I'll walk you to your car."

She'd expected the offer. Carlo was a thoughtful, considerate man. For example, those business cards...

With quick steps she took herself into his office. "You had cards made for me."

He looked up, obviously puzzled. "Yeah."

"You had them made before today's meeting."

"And this is news because..."

"You...you were willing to lay claim to me as a McMillan & Milano employee even before you saw how I handled the meeting."

He shook his head. "Lucy, you *are* a McMillan & Milano employee, and of course I assumed you'd handle the meeting well. You're a very capable person."

"But...but..."

"Claudia took me aside before we left to say that very thing to me. The words she used, I believe, were that she should know by now not to underestimate anyone, even little blondies like you."

Lucy laughed, unable to work up the least bit of mad at the "little blondie" remark. Yes, it made her sound like a new brand of cookie or some kind of candy, but who cared? The fact was, flush with success and the recognition for that success, she felt like dancing. And so she did. She danced right around the desk, wearing a grin so wide she could see it in the reflection of the window behind Carlo.

After all, she *had* proved she was competent. Capable. Claudia thought so. Carlo said so. Better yet, *Lucy* knew so.

And at that happy thought, she leaned down and gave her temporary boss a great big smack.

On the mouth.

Chapter Five

Uh-oh. The kiss changed on contact. What she'd intended to be a grateful, happy smack, turned downright serious when her lips touched Carlo's. His hands gripped her waist and pulled her down into his lap.

Her head found the hollow of his shoulder as she tilted her chin to give him fuller access. And oh, he accepted the invitation. His tongue slid against hers, dominant and sure. She opened her mouth wider, taking every thrust as her body began to hum from head to toes, more sensitive spots along the way beginning their own heavy throb.

His hand, hot and big, inched upward from her hip and anticipation robbed the last of her breath. *Yes, yes,* she urged him silently, aroused just by the kiss. *Now touch me there. Touch me again there.*

Millimeters short, his wandering fingers froze. His kiss eased. "Goose," he groaned against her mouth, then lifted his head and let his hand drop away.

Without his mouth on hers, Lucy managed to assess the situation. Here they were, both breathing hard, both obviously affected—that was *not* a banana she could feel against the pocket beneath her hip—but one of them was regretting the position they were in. The other only wanted it to go on and on and on.

She swallowed and put off the moment where she'd be forced off his lap simply by pretending she wasn't sitting there. Maybe if she talked about something else, they'd avoid talking about this. She didn't want it once again labeled "forgettable."

"So," she started, as if they were separated by the desk instead of less than five layers of cloth, "you really think I handled the meeting competently? I thought the volunteers looked pleased with me, as well."

Her strategy appeared to work, because while Carlo frowned, he didn't lift her away. "Particularly that guy wearing the Torrey Pines Golf Course shirt. He asked me about you. Whether you were available."

"Really?" Blinking, Lucy drew back to get a better look at Carlo's face and he circled his hands to the small of her back to keep her from falling off his knees. Nice. "I don't remember a man in a Torrey Pines Golf Course shirt," she said.

"He was the one with the gold Rolex and the preoccupation with your breasts."

Just that word out of Carlo's mouth sent a sexual zap up Lucy's spine. She squirmed against his thighs and his hold on her reflexively tightened. "He couldn't see my br— You know," she protested. Not when covered with her mortuary-appropriate suit jacket.

"Maybe he has X-ray vision." As if he might, as well, Carlo's gaze flickered from her face to her chest, and in a rush her nipples contracted inside her bra. Could he tell? The sleeveless blouse she was wearing was of a thin, delicate white cotton with horizontal rows of lace bisected by the placket of tiny pearl buttons.

Lucy swallowed again, feeling a flush rise to her skin. "You…" She had to start again, her throat was so dry. "You told him I was single?"

Carlo's eyes widened. His look seemed to suggest she was insane.

Maybe she was. Because she thought he looked a little possessive, too…and still a lot turned on. One of her hands toyed with the knot of his navy-blue-and-red tie, and she found herself working at loosening it. "By the way, I noticed one of the group giving you the eye, too," she told him, breathless again. The ends of the tie fell loose and she even went so far as to unfasten the button at his collar.

Bad Lucy, she told herself, peeking at him from beneath her lashes. Bad, flirtatious Lucy. But she couldn't seem to halt her daring. "Though I think the woman was more than a little wary of this serious, buttoned-up look of yours."

"Was it the redhead with the large hoop earrings?"

There'd been a redhead with large hoop earrings? "Um, I…" She'd been making the whole thing up. Truth to tell, she'd been too nervous about the meeting itself to absorb those kinds of details about the people in attendance.

"You know," he went on, "the one who wrote her phone number on your business card and passed it over to me."

Lucy's jaw dropped and she sat up straighter. "Some pushy redhead used *my* business card to come on to you?" She flounced and felt her eyebrows lower. "That is so rude."

"She even crossed out your name so I could see hers more clearly."

So incredibly rude!

Carlo made a sound that was suspiciously like a stifled laugh. "Oh, God." He made that sound again. "You should see the expression on your face."

"What?"

He put a hand over his mouth, but nothing smothered the sound of his laughter now. And while Lucy loved seeing this unusual sign of his good humor, it wasn't so great when it was at her expense.

And what was wrong with her expression, anyway? Annoyed as he continued to laugh, she shifted on his lap so that her knees straddled either side of his thighs. Placing her hands on the back of his leather executive chair, she kneeled up to check out her reflection in the window behind him.

Okay, her expression did appear a bit…peeved, but it was all his fault. He'd—

"Oh, Lucy." His laughter had died and he groaned now, his hands clamping around her waist and then sliding toward her breasts. "Lucy, how you tempt me. Every day. Every hour."

His touch, the unwilling need in his voice, tempted her, too. Kneeling up had placed her breasts at the level of his face and she had to wonder if her surprising inner self—that flirtatious, naughty, surprising inner self— had planned it all along. Her heart pounded loud in her ears as his hands inched farther upward, closing gently over her breasts. She could feel his breath, hot, through the thin cotton of her shirt.

"Carlo," she whispered.

"I'm not supposed to want this." His palms gave her a gentle caress.

At the exquisite touch, her lashes drifted down. Through half-closed eyes, she could still see her reflection. As she watched, as he continued to circle and stroke, her nostrils flared and her mouth parted, clearly expressing her excitement. Hunger. Want.

"Carlo," she said again, her hands clutching the chair's black leather. "Please."

His breath blew hot across one nipple, then he latched on to it through her blouse and her bra. Her body shuddered. She'd never, ever felt like this. So quickly. So hot. So needy. "Please don't stop."

He didn't let up the arousing caress, and she wanted to cry at how perfect it was. Then he lifted his head and she moaned in protest.

"Shh, shh," he soothed, as his fingers made short work of her buttons. He brushed the blouse off her shoulders and neither of them minded that it was still caught in the waistband of her skirt. Carlo's hands were as competent with the front clasp of her bra as they were with every-thing else. Then that garment was gone and he found her neglected breast, running his mouth over every inch of the plump, aching skin—except the inch that needed him most.

Her fingers flexed in the leather, but then she couldn't stand it anymore. Grasping his head between her hands, she placed him right where she wanted him.

He let out a short, satisfied laugh, and then he took her into his mouth. She bowed into the sweet, hot suction and her thighs trembled with each deliberate pull.

His touch wasn't gentle, not like the first kiss at the Street Beat party. It was strong enough to signal that this was a man who knew how to please her, a man who was making manly demands, and the temperature of her blood rose along with each one of them. His hands roamed over the bare skin of her back, then along her hips and back up again. The hem of her skirt, already hiked up thanks to her kneeling position, caught on his wrists and rode higher as his palms discovered the tops of her thigh-high stockings and the bare skin of her hips.

His head lifted from her breast to peer down at the flesh in his hands. "Hell, Lucy. Hell…"

The rasp of his breath and the dazed look in her eyes let her know he was as affected, as aroused as she. It gave her confidence. Even sass.

"What did you expect?" she asked. "Granny panties?" She backed off the chair to stand on the floor between his splayed thighs, her heart slamming against her chest.

Her flirtatious courage amazed her. Who was this Lucy? This Lucy whose blood was pounding so fast through her system that she felt dizzy with lust? Who was this Lucy who coolly reached behind her to locate the top button of her skirt? This Lucy who let the lined, pin-striped garment drop, taking along with it her blouse. This Lucy who stood before the man she'd been crushing on for what seemed like centuries in a nude-colored thong, nude stockings held up by a wide band of black stretch lace, and wearing black high heels.

This Lucy who loved the poleaxed look on Carlo Milano's face and who had the nerve to take the ends of his tie in one fist and draw him up from the chair. "Wouldn't the couch be more comfortable?"

He followed like a zombie.

Like a besotted lover.

Like a man under a spell that was the same as the one bewitching Lucy. He was the perfect follower, the perfect cobewitchee, until she hesitated by the leather couch. Then he seemed to find his will again, and it caused him to strip off his shirt, then take Lucy in his arms only to drop her onto the couch.

She gasped at the cold against her bare back and bare bottom, but he filled her open mouth with his tongue as he followed her down. He warmed her with the heat of his naked chest. Her heart slammed hard against his, and she opened her thighs to help him settle deeper into the cradle of her pelvis.

At the contact, they both groaned and took the kiss deeper. When she was desperate for breath, he lifted his head and looked down into her eyes as he brushed the hair off her face. The gesture was so tender and made her feel so cherished that this time she felt actual tears sting the corners of her eyes.

Carlo froze. "Oh, Lucy." His lashes swept down and she saw him clench his jaw. "Oh, Goose."

Oh, no.

Don't do this. Please, Carlo, don't stop now.

Desperate to avoid what was coming next, she tried her strategy again. "So," she started, then stopped to steady her voice. "So, you really think I handled that meeting well?"

She scrutinized his face, anxious to see his expression ease from regret to…what? Could she truly hope to turn his thoughts to desire once again?

His lips gave a wry twist. "Not going to work this time, Goose."

Someday, Lucy was going to think of a punishment fitting enough for her oldest sibling, who was responsible for her irritating nickname. The family tried to fob it off, claiming that Jason couldn't say her name clearly and "Goosey" was his mangled form of Lucy. Right. He'd been nine when she was born and was now an eloquent trial attorney. He'd never had trouble talking.

She ran through a series of tortures as Carlo levered himself off the couch and then snagged his dress shirt from the floor. His touch was impersonal as he helped her sit and then pushed her arms into his sleeves.

His gaze focused on the buttons, and he nimbly fastened the shirt.

"You seem to be making a habit of that," she said, sounding truculent yet not giving a damn about it.

He didn't look up. "Buttoning? Unbuttoning? Kissing you? Stopping kissing you?"

"Regretting kissing me." She'd hoped to say it silently, but what the hey.

Carlo's breath came out on a long sigh, and then he sat down beside her on the couch. "Goose—"

"*Lucy.*"

He nodded. "Right, right. *Lucy.* It's just that thinking of you as Goose…it…"

"It makes me sound as if I'm eight years old. And I'm not eight years old, Carlo. I'm a woman."

"I know that."

"A grown woman."

He passed a hand over his face. "Where do you think this crazy sexual chemistry comes from? Obviously I know you're a woman."

"Well, what? What's the problem, then?" she demanded. "You made a date with the redhead and you're afraid you'll be late?"

Unbelievably, Carlo laughed again. Then he took a look at her face and sobered. "G— Lucy, that's exactly why we can't take this path."

"You actually *do* have a date?"

"No. And there wasn't any redhead, either. But it was so damn fun to tease you about it. I can't mess with that."

She remembered his laughter and how much it had thrilled her to see serious, all-business Carlo amused and letting it show. Still… "I don't like being the butt of your jokes."

"You know you weren't." He gave a brotherly pinch

to her chin. "It's just that...that...Lucy, for the past few days you've been the sun around here."

Why didn't that sound promising?

"You're bright and sparkling and you warm this place up. I...I suppose sometimes I need that."

Lucy's heart fluttered. Had he just said he needed her?

"But too close, sweetheart, too close and the sun will burn. I'll burn *you*, Lucy, and I can't have that."

He meant he wouldn't have *her*. Because he didn't do the couple thing, which he'd said from the beginning, which she'd known for years. Another man would have let them be swept out on the tide of lust and to hell with the consequences, but not Carlo.

Damn him.

Okay.

Not damn him.

Didn't you have a crush on a noble, upstanding guy precisely because he *was* so noble?

Carlo picked up her hand and held it in a loose grasp. "Goose, I enjoy having you here. I'm glad there're a couple more weeks that you'll be around the office and we'll be together. But not like this. I need your friendship, long-term, way more than this kind of indulgence."

She opened her mouth to protest. They could indulge, couldn't they? What was wrong with a no-strings fling? She *wanted* to indulge.

But that wasn't a good enough reason, she conceded. Not with all the connections between their families that a casual affair might mess up. There'd be a million future moments that wouldn't be made better with a stilted goodbye between them. Not to mention his long-held feelings for her sister...

And anyway, Lucy had come here to get over her crush!

A woman who read *Cosmo* or who lived vicariously through soap operas or friends' love lives—which sometimes had strikingly eerie parallels—knew you couldn't fling someone out of your system. She had a crush on Carlo and was working here with him in order to crush *it*, not nurture the inconvenient feelings with naked kisses and caresses.

She sighed, then flopped against the back of the couch. "Okay." Withdrawing her fingers from his, she patted the back of his hand. "Okay, you're right."

He looked relieved, and she tried to be fine with that. Maybe it would be best if she resigned from McMillan & Milano, she thought. Put up with the guff she would be sure to get from her nosy family for leaving yet another job. It would be the easiest way to avoid having to be with this beautiful, maddening man—*you're the sun, Lucy*—every day.

But there was that. That, *you're the sun, Lucy*. Despite everything, she liked the idea that she could bring light to Carlo's darkness. He'd lingered in the shadows for far too long.

"Friends, Goose?"

If it kills me.

The hours at McMillan & Milano were going to be the thing that killed Lucy. Not only was there the regular work week, but she had grabbed at the offered overtime and came in on Saturday. Though she could use the extra money, by the afternoon she was exhausted, sick of the same walls around her, and even then she didn't look half as burned out as her temporary boss.

As she brought Carlo the umpteenth cup of coffee, she couldn't help but notice his blank stare at the layout spread across his desk. It was the design of the Street Beat festival venue, with its five stages, food areas, first aid and bathroom facilities. In previous years, Street Beat had been shoehorned into the busy, revitalized downtown area—"a security nightmare," according to Carlo—but it didn't look like the festival's relocation to the parking lot of the football stadium was making the head of security sleep any better.

Without the cramped quarters constraining the ticket sales, the expected attendance—and presumably the nightmare factor—had gone way up.

Lucy set the mug down on the corner of his desk. He didn't even grunt his thanks as he usually did. She wondered for a second if he was asleep with his eyes open.

"Are you even seeing that?"

"Seeing what?" he mumbled, without glancing up.

She was used to that. In the days since their passionate interlude in that very chair, in this very office, Carlo had done his best not to catch her eye. One time he had, his gaze meeting hers as she brought in a stack of reports, and it had all rushed back.

His mouth on her breast.

His hot, rough palms on her naked hips.

The tenderness of his touch.

You're the sun, Lucy.

But since then it had all been business.

How could she warm him, make him smile, if the man who'd had business cards made up for her wouldn't let himself look her in the face?

"Let's get out of here," she said.

"What?" He lifted his gaze to her left shoulder.

She bent her knees so that it was her eyes he was seeing instead. "We've been inside here too long. Let's go to the beach."

"Huh?"

"You know. That place with sand and ocean. The reason so many people choose San Diego to live. You're not getting anything done here. I'm giving myself paper cuts due to claustrophobia."

He blinked, looked concerned. "You've hurt yourself?"

She shook her head. "Lack of fresh air is making you dumb if you can't discern hyperbole when you hear it. But okay, yeah, I've hurt myself and the only cure is you let me take you to the beach."

It surprised the heck out of her when he rose from his chair. "You're right. We both need a break."

But she should have known it wouldn't be that easy. When they reached the parking garage, he peeled off toward his car.

"Carlo!"

"I won't leave until I make sure your car starts."

Lucy rolled her eyes and stomped over to him and grabbed him by the elbow. "This way. My car. Me and you. The beach." His feet dragged against the concrete.

"Goose…"

"You called me that name again. You owe me for that alone." Then they were at her Volkswagen Bug and she was stuffing him into the passenger seat.

"I don't fit in here," he protested as she pushed on his knees to fold them further.

"Stop complaining."

He didn't. Though he wasn't loud about it, he did continue to mutter. He even heaved a sigh as they came to a stop in the parking lot of Belmont Park, the amusement area alongside Mission Beach.

His eagerness to get out of the car wasn't as gratifying as it might have been when he unpretzeled himself from his seat. "Five more minutes and you could serve me with mustard," he said, giving her a squinty glare.

The comment made her feel hungry, not guilty. So their first stop was the ice cream shop, where, as they were waiting in line, she caught him pulling out his cell phone.

"Give me that," she ordered, snatching it away and slipping it into the front pocket of her jeans. "You need a break, you take a break."

He rolled his eyes this time but paid for their cones and then followed her onto the boardwalk. They strolled among others enjoying the beautiful autumn day, dodging skateboards and bicycles, and zigzagging around little kids dragging plastic buckets of shells. Lucy sucked in big lungfuls of air between long licks of her rocky road ice cream.

Tongue out, she caught Carlo studying her over his pralines and cream. She lowered her cone. "What?"

He shrugged. "I was just trying to calculate how long it's been since I've hung out at the beach."

"Too long."

"Yeah." His head turned and he stared out at the water. "My dad used to bring my brothers and sister and me here all the time."

"Brave man." Carlo was the youngest of four brothers; his sister, Francesca, was younger than him.

"We were hellions. Our favorite trick was to convince Franny to catch seagulls."

Lucy had never heard about that. "Catch seagulls? How do you do that?"

"We'd dig a hole big enough for Franny to lie in. Then we'd cover her with a beach towel and cover *that* with corn chips. When the gulls swooped down for the bait, she was supposed to swoop up and trap them inside the towel."

Lucy blinked. "And she would actually do this?"

"For an ice cream cone and the promise that we'd play school with her later."

"Oh, and I bet that happened." Lucy knew all about the promises of elder siblings.

"We did play with her. But we always acted up enough so that Teacher Franny sent us home early." He grinned. "I haven't thought about all that in ages."

They walked a little farther, then turned back toward the amusement area. "My sister and brothers wouldn't play my games," Lucy said. "And included me in theirs only under great duress."

"Even Elise?"

She shot him a sidelong glance. "Perfect Elise wasn't always so perfect, you know."

His neutral expression didn't change. "Who said she was?" As they passed a trash can, he threw away the remains of his cone. "I only thought as the other girl in the family she'd do girly things with you."

"Nope. You should remember that all my sibs were manic about board games. They'd play marathons of word games. Imagine me, Lucy, trying to compete with Jason and Sam and Elise. They're all enough older that they could count better, spell better, and had vocabularies that included *attorney* and *financier* and *actuary*."

Carlo laughed at her bitterness. "Funny, how they then came to choose those professions."

"Yeah, and this when I was at the stage where I wanted to grow up and raise magic ponies." Her brothers and sister still teased her about it. If you opened any old game box at her parents' house, you'd still find the old tallies. Years and years of Lucy coming in last. "So in the game department, Goose always earned the big goose-egg score."

Carlo wrapped his arm around her neck and drew her against his chest in a hug that was all about affection and nothing about seduction. "But you're working your magic now, Luce." He smiled down at her and his teeth were even whiter in contrast to his weekend stubble. "Who else could have enticed me away from my desk and then dragged me to the beach for an ice cream cone and a ride on the roller coaster?"

"Ride on the roller coaster?" Lucy hoped her voice didn't squeak, and she also hoped he couldn't tell she was trying to hang back as he directed the two of them toward the line for the old-time wooden ride, the Big Dipper. "We don't have to do the roller coaster."

His grin only widened and the sunlight was sparkling in his dark eyes. "Make me happy, Luce."

Make him laugh, is what he meant, she thought, recognizing the dare in his eyes. Hadn't she grown up with brothers? Hadn't he just told her about the way he'd get his little sister to let herself be seagull bait?

She slipped out of his hold and stomped to the end of the line. "Don't whine to me if you get a stomachache."

Behind her, his free-and-easy laugh made the flutters in her own belly worthwhile. If she was his sun, then his laughter was the bubbles in her champagne. Being with him like this—Carlo relaxed and funny and comfortable—made *her* happy.

Not happy enough to override her nerves when they were shown their seats in the coaster. Pasting a cheerful smile on her face, she made enough room for him so that she couldn't even take comfort from his warmth. She didn't need it, she told herself.

"This is going to be fantastic fun!" She hoped she wasn't lying.

Carlo glanced down at her and grinned again. The ocean breeze ruffled the edges of his businesslike haircut and made him look ten years younger. Before Elise had broken his heart. Before his partner had died.

"Lucy," he said. "I can't remember the last time I've had such a great afternoon."

Short of expiring from fright, nothing could take away from that perfect moment. Carlo's handsome face. Carlo's *carefree* and handsome face. The smile that he was beaming down at her, and at her alone.

She hung on to that perfection as the car lurched into motion. Her smile was pinned at both corners by pure determination as they started the climb. With luck, he wouldn't notice her white knuckles clamped around the restraining bar.

They'd almost reached the top. Lucy's eyeballs felt cold and as wide as the pit in her belly. She didn't like heights. She detested fast roller coasters. She hated the sense of falling, so much that she avoided elevators whenever reasonably possible.

But she couldn't ruin Carlo's wild ride.

There was that horrid suspended moment at the top and then they were falling, speeding, rushing. In the car behind them, someone was screaming over and over.

Lucy dug her fingernails into the metal lap bar and kept a determined hold of her rigor mortis grin. Until Carlo reached out and wrapped her shoulders with his arm. He pulled her close. "Wha...?" She looked up, trying to say something over the scary, rushing wind.

His mouth tickled her ear. "I need somebody to hang on to." And then he tucked her closer against his chest and she surrendered to her fears. Burying her face at his throat, she clung to him through the next thirty-seven years of her life.

Later, he told her it was more like thirty-seven seconds. But that was when her feet were on solid ground and she could appreciate that she'd survived. She could also appreciate that glimmering light in his eyes and that smile of his that didn't show a single sign of dimming.

An odd chirping from deep in her pants pocket interrupted her self-congratulation. When she realized it was Carlo's cell phone, she would have liked to have ignored it, but he was already putting out his hand.

So what? she thought, drawing it out. His shoulders were relaxed, his lips were still curved, he still looked happy. And it was all thanks to Lucy.

He flipped it open and held it to his ear.

At a public-safety demonstration, Lucy had once watched a man use a blanket to smother a fire. It was like that now with Carlo's expression. All that was glowing with life was gone in an instant.

It was as though nothing warm had ever existed.

Chapter Six

As he folded his cell phone closed, Carlo grabbed Lucy's hand and tugged her in the direction of the parking lot. It was still bright enough for sunglasses, but he didn't feel the sun's warmth. A little kid ran across their path and the child's vivid red shorts and neon-orange T-shirt hurt his eyes. Teenagers off to the right were laughing and the sound rang too loudly in his ears.

Even the smiles on the people he passed in his hurry to reach the parking lot felt wrong. It seemed as if a dark well had opened up in his gut and sucked down everything good about the day.

"Carlo? Carlo, what is it?" There was an edge to Lucy's voice.

Gritting his teeth, he shortened his stride so he

wasn't dragging her behind him. *Keep it together, Milano. You won't help anyone by losing your cool.*

"Carlo?"

"It's Germaine." He schooled his features so they betrayed nothing as he glanced down at Lucy. Their afternoon's adventure had delivered a slight sunburn across her cheeks and a light sprinkle of freckles on her nose. She was so damn pretty. So damn sweet. For a minute he wished he could run away with her, go some place far away where there was no darkness and nothing to worry about besides finding ways to make her eyes sparkle and that rosebud mouth of hers to curve in happiness.

"Carlo?"

He shook away the little fantasy. "Germaine had a fall. Or maybe worse. Her neighbor caught sight of her lying on her front walk and called 911, and then called her sister and me."

Lucy's hand tightened on his. "Why didn't you say so right away? Let's go." She picked up her speed, now tugging him. "I know the hospital nearest her house."

He had to go there, of course. He was practically the closest thing she had to family, now that Pat was gone.

Pat. At the thought of his old partner, Carlo's footsteps slowed, but Lucy was having none of it. "Come on," she said, yanking on his hand.

He forced himself forward. *Keep it together, Milano. Keep it cool.* Lucy didn't need to know how this was going to cost him. Lucy wouldn't know, because he'd send her on her way first. Walking into the hospital would set off a rockslide of memories, but he'd be alone with them. Maybe not better equipped to handle their impact, but at least without a witness to their damage.

Lucy didn't prove so easy to shake. At the hospital, she zipped past the hospital entrance and sped toward the parking area without giving even a token tap on the brake pedal when he protested.

"Just drop me off at the front," he told her. "I'll catch a ride home by calling a cab or one of my brothers or something."

Her little Bug whipped into a narrow parking space. "Germaine needs you. You need a friend."

He stared at her and dumbly repeated her words. "I need a friend?"

"Everybody needs a friend," she asserted, and exited the car with brisk movements. "We're buddies, right?"

"Bosom buddies," he muttered, following in her wake. For someone so short she could cover distances in an amazingly brief amount of time. He watched the plate-glass entrance doors automatically whisk open as her running shoes hit the black rubber mat. From his place on the sidewalk, he watched them close behind her. Six steps toward the front desk, he saw her register that he'd remained outside.

She flitted back out the doors. "Are you okay?"

No. Not okay. That pit in his gut had now been filled with boulders and branches and broken pieces of glass that were churning and turning and tearing at his insides.

But that was his private pain. Taking a breath, he started forward. "I'm coming. I was just…thinking."

Thinking too much. Remembering.

Keep it together!

The doors opened again and seemed to draw them inward along with some of the odors of the world outside: warm asphalt, grass newly mowed, the acrid exhaust of a laundry truck. And then the plate glass closed behind them and the outside world and its scents disappeared, leaving Carlo trapped in this other world that smelled of cold equipment, old magazines, desperate hopes.

Lucy was heading off toward the front desk again, but Carlo snagged her arm. "E.R.," he said. "I know how to get there."

She shot him a strange look, which made him guess that he sounded as strangled as he felt. He cleared his throat. "Lucy. Look. You go on home. I've got things covered."

"Sure you do," she answered, but she was walking again, this time in the direction of the emergency room.

He glared at her back in mounting frustration as he followed behind her. "Lucy, go home." Damn it, she was going to make him nuts and he wasn't in any shape to fight it, not when every inhalation of what the hospital called "air" made him think of the night they'd brought in Pat. Even without closing his eyes he could see the stain spreading on his partner's sleeve from beneath his bulletproof vest. Blood bubbling from his mouth and running over the silvery five o'clock shadow on the older man's chin.

Without thinking, Carlo reached out to stroke the back of Lucy's sunny hair. It was the color of butter and felt like that, too, smooth and soft. The picture in his head of Pat receded. "I don't need you, Lucy," he said, even as he twined his fingers in her blond strands. "I don't."

"You won't even know I'm here," she assured him.

Of course, that was a big lie. He'd known exactly where she was for days, ever since she'd showed up to temp at McMillan & Milano. He'd been hyperaware of her every glance, every small sharp intake of breath, every response she'd had to his kisses and to his touch. Even as hours passed and despite his worry for Germaine and those debilitating memories lurking in the corners of his mind, he was still aware of Lucy. She'd found a chair in the corner of the E.R. waiting room and had drawn up her legs to curl herself into its molded plastic.

Though he tried pretending she wasn't there, her steady gaze kept him from snapping at the E.R. receptionist when she refused to give him any information. It kept his voice calm when he recognized a doctor from his police-department days and asked for news. It was Lucy who nudged him when an older woman entered the waiting area. She'd guessed it was Germaine's sister, Dot, and she was right.

As the late afternoon wore into the evening, then into late evening, they learned that Germaine was stable for the moment, but was being X-rayed for possible fractures. The doctor had yet to rule out a stroke as the cause of her fall. Lucy kept up the supply of coffee and tea for Carlo and Dot, but the caffeine didn't help his mood.

God, all this waiting! Those around them shifted and changed. A baby with a heavy cough was finally seen. A grizzled old man held his arm against his chest at an odd angle but was stoic, his eyes closed, as he waited for his name to be called. Everything took so damn long in a hospital, Carlo thought.

"I wish Pat were here," Dot suddenly said.

Carlo's belly churned. "Yeah." Instead, Germaine was alone.

Carlo was alone.

He didn't remember getting to his feet. He didn't decide to do it. One moment he was staring into the black depths of his coffee, the next he was making strides for the nearest exit.

Can't stand the smell. Can't stand the memories.

Pat on a gurney, his eyes already glazed behind slitted lids. At noon that day, Carlo and his partner had eaten lunch with Germaine in their kitchen. Over the meal, the older couple had talked about their plans following Pat's retirement from the police force. He and Carlo were already well on their way to opening the security firm, but Pat had promised Germaine a cruise before getting too caught up in the new venture. They'd eaten sloppy joes and green salad that Germaine had prepared, and they'd been back at their desks before Pat noticed the sauce stain on his tie.

Pat had shaken his head. "Germaine's gonna kill me. She gave me this tie for my birthday."

Germaine hadn't killed him. That had been the prerogative of a gangbanger with a loose trigger finger. And the sloppy joe stain on Pat's tie had been swallowed by the much larger stain made by Pat's blood.

As he thought of Pat's death, the walls of the hospital

hallway squeezed his chest, pressing the air out of Carlo's lungs. Breathless, he was forced to sag against the nearest plaster surface to keep from passing out. Wouldn't that be a pretty sight? Former cop made faint by nothing more than his own bad memories. He was so damn weak, he thought, pushing the heels of his hands against his eyes. Some things made him so damn weak.

"Carlo."

Damn.

Lucy's voice. Lucy.

He dropped his hands and turned toward her, willing his spine to stay straight and hoping like hell the panic was gone from his eyes. When she came nearer, he slapped on a scowl as a preemptive strike. "I told you to go home, didn't I? I wish you'd go home."

I never want you to see me like this.

"Oh, be quiet."

He stared at her, startled by her no-nonsense tone. "What?"

"I have older brothers, you know. And Elise, despite what you think, could be a royal bitch, especially between the years of thirteen to fifteen. So I don't scare off easily."

He hated how she saw through him. Hadn't the same thing happened the night of the Street Beat party? It ticked him off now, it did. His own siblings and father knew when to back off. Why didn't Lucy? "Look. I just want you to go—"

"Away. I get that. Well, we're both going to get your wish, because the doctor just came out and told Dot they're admitting Germaine. They have a room for her on the fourth floor. Dot's staying with her."

"Can I see—"

But Lucy was already shaking her head. "It's just overnight, but they've given Germaine something to help her rest. Nothing's broken and they've stitched up the cut on her head. I think they're only keeping her because of her age and the lateness of the hour. Or maybe your buddy the E.R. doc said something. Anyway, it looks as if it was a simple slip and fall with no major lasting effects."

A simple slip and fall that wouldn't have happened if Pat were still...

He needed to stop thinking about Pat. "All right. Okay. Let's say goodbye to Dot and get out of here."

As he'd hoped, the fresh night air helped. And by the time Lucy braked in front of his house, he could think of something besides Germaine's fall and Pat's tragic death. Like how he'd been a hell of a lousy companion the past few hours.

With a sigh, he glanced over at Lucy. "I owe you a beer for all you've done today. Will you come inside? Maybe I can scrounge up some food, as well."

She hesitated. "I should probably let you get some rest. It's been a rough day for you and—"

"There's nothing wrong with me!" It came out more defensive than he would have liked, but her solicitude wasn't necessary. "I'm fine. Come in, damn it."

"Well, when you put it so nicely..." With a roll of her eyes, she turned off the car then followed him inside. "I guess I could use a beer."

Once in his kitchen, he kind of shoved a bottle at her, but she took it without comment and pulled out a chair to seat herself at his breakfast table. He turned back to the refrigerator, feeling more of his anxiety fall away as he studied the familiar—meager—contents of the shelves. "We have cold pizza, and cold pizza, and some leftover cold Chinese, not to mention cold—"

The sound of glass breaking spun him around.

"Oh, I'm such a klutz!" Lucy dropped to her knees near a puddle of beer and began picking up shards of the bottle. "This will just take a second," she said, glancing up. "Get me some paper towels, will you?"

He turned away to comply, then turned back. "Here."

She glanced over her shoulder at him as her fingers found another piece of glass. It must have slipped, or been sharper than she expected, because suddenly blood welled from her fingers. A cut, he thought, going cold as he stared at the fresh red. She'd cut herself, and she'd yet to feel it.

From the corners of his mind, anxiety seeped like a dark cloud. His muscles froze though his stomach roiled as drops of shocking red splashed against the tiled floor. Lucy was still looking at him and her eyes widened at whatever expression crossed his face.

She dropped the piece of glass and rose to her feet, lifting that bloody hand to her face to stroke away a piece of hair clinging to her cheek at the same time. The movement left a smear of crimson slashing from the corner of her mouth to the edge of her chin.

The dark smoke billowed, obscuring the line between reality and memory. Lucy's cut. Pat's wound. Lucy. Pat.

"We have to stop the blood," he heard himself

saying. "Right away. Gotta stop the blood." He had Lucy's hand now, and was holding the paper towels against the cut, applying pressure to the slice even as he scrubbed at the blood on her face with another towel he ripped from the roll. "Gotta stop the blood."

Dread tightened his chest as he stared down at the paper towels wrapped around the cut. The red stain on them was spreading outward, getting larger by the second. In his mind, the towels morphed into his partner's shirtsleeve, going dark and heavy with the liquid pumping from beneath his vest. The dark blue shirt appeared black.

"So much blood, Pat," he heard himself mutter. "Too much blood."

"Carlo."

From far away, a voice was calling his name. He tried to shake it off—he didn't have time to answer, he had to do something about all this blood or else Pat was going to bleed to death before his eyes—but now there was someone tugging on his sleeve.

"Carlo. Carlo, I'm okay. The bleeding's stopped. It's just a little cut."

Lucy's voice. Lucy's hand. He looked up. Lucy's concerned face. Not Pat. Pat was gone.

His head cleared. The past faded and the dread that had been squeezing Carlo's chest was replaced with heat. The heat of humiliation.

And anger. Anger at himself for not keeping it together. Anger at Lucy—and God, he knew it was unfair, but he was angry at her all the same—for being there to watch him lose it.

She had to think he was nuts. Her free hand stroked his shoulder and there was sympathy in her eyes.

She *did* think he was nuts.

But she didn't run out of the house screaming. Instead, she stroked his arm again. "Maybe..." She licked her lips. "Maybe you should see someone."

"No." Now she was really making him mad. Couldn't she leave well enough alone? This was his little neurosis, and it wasn't hers to comment upon. He didn't want to hear her say he should see a shrink. He didn't want to discuss his crazy little flashbacks.

"Carlo. You could talk—"

"*No.*"

"Talk about—"

She wouldn't shut up. So he did it for her, he shut her up by pulling her close and stopping the conversation by putting his mouth on hers. Hard.

It was punishment, Lucy knew that. Punishment for Carlo being understandably affected by his partner's widow's hospitalization and punishment for Lucy being the one to see that effect.

But she clung to him, offering her kiss and offering comfort, because she understood what today had cost him. And she'd do what she had to—as a friend, okay?—to take that tragedy out of his eyes.

His arm scooped around her hips and brought her closer against his. She felt him harden against her belly as his tongue entered her mouth. At the first thrust, thoughts of comfort evaporated as goose bumps swept across her skin in a hot rush.

Oh.

Her body bowed into his and her friendly intentions were run off by the sensation of his hot hands squeezing her bottom and his mouth moving against hers. She crowded closer to him, and let her tongue tangle with his. Her eyes closed.

Then he broke their kiss, muttering something. Though his hold on her was as strong as before, he merely rested his forehead against hers. Their ragged breathing matched, but she knew the expression in her eyes wasn't anywhere near as sad as his.

Noble Carlo, once again in deep regret.

"I'm sorry," he said a moment later, confirming that she'd pegged his reaction exactly right. "Sorry *again.* Damn it, I keep ending up like this with you when I don't mean to."

At least he hadn't said it wasn't where he *wanted* to be, though she supposed the erection she could still feel pressed against her made that point moot.

He inhaled a long breath. "What *is* it about you?"

His expression twisted her heart. She wished she could do something about that. What had Elise said to her? That Carlo needed to lighten up. That Lucy should make that part of her job description.

He frowned down at her. "Why do you keep getting past my best intentions, Goose?"

So serious. So worried. *I don't think he knows how to have fun.* Lucy replayed her sister's words again. Maybe it was time Lucy reminded him of what that was like. Maybe it was time to bring him a little more sunshine.

"Will you forgive me, Goose?"

"That's the last straw," Lucy said, taking matters in her mental hands as she stepped back from him. "I mean it." She pointed her finger at him. "Strip."

He stared. "What?"

"You heard me. I said strip." She gave him the no-nonsense eye. "I warned you that the next time you called me Goose that you'd owe me, big time, and you agreed."

Had he? It didn't matter. Lucy tapped a toe, signaling impatience. "So now I'm collecting. Take off your clothes."

"What?"

"That wasn't the first time you got me all worked up only to leave me hanging. I'm not taking it anymore. Now I'm demanding. I'm demanding uh...uh... I'm demanding a Carlo sundae." Inspired by her own impulsive words, she moved toward the refrigerator. "Surely you have some chocolate sauce and whipped cream in here."

Though she didn't look at him as she rummaged around in the refrigerator, she hoped like heck that her outrageousness would change the atmosphere in the room. Her fingers closed around a metal canister.

"Is this all you have?" she demanded, spinning back to face him. "Because I'll make do, but Cheez Whiz is not my first choice."

His arms were folded over his chest. His expression was bemused, a vast improvement over bleak, though there wasn't yet a sparkle of humor. "What the hell are you doing?"

"Complaining about the contents of your refrigerator." She looked back inside and pounced on another item tucked behind a bottle of salad dressing. "Uh-oh. This is chocolate whipped cream."

She slammed the door shut with her hip. "I'm a little miffed about this. Chocolate whipped cream is not a guy thing. It's an item only a woman would buy. Have you been making man sundaes for some other girl?"

He was shaking his head, looking at her as if she was the one who needed a shrink, so she flitted over, can in hand. "Hey, but if it's this or the Cheez Whiz, I guess I'll take the cream."

Toe to toe with him, she arched an eyebrow as she tossed the cap on the counter and shook the can. "Why are your clothes still on?"

He huffed out a breath. "You are not going to get near me with that stuff."

She hadn't grown up the youngest for nothing. She poked his belly with the cold can. "I'm near." Then she nudged his forearm with it. "And look. Near again."

When she reached farther upward he grabbed her hand. "Knock it off," he said, wearing a fierce frown. "What are you doing?"

Didn't anyone ever tease him anymore? She fought to gain back control of the can, but his hold tightened, and then suddenly it sprayed, scattering a flurry of chocolate whipped cream across his beige shirt.

They both stared at the mess. "Whoops," Lucy said, and let loose a little snicker. "Now you really will have to take it off."

"Look what you've done."

"Oh, please, Carlo. Take it off and I'll run cold water over it and it will be as good as new." Maybe.

But at least he didn't look sad anymore as he lifted off the shirt and handed it over. Annoyed was an improvement, in her mind. Still, not what she'd been going for.

And so, well, it was another impulse. As she took the shirt with her left hand, the trigger finger on her right just happened to create a tiny chocolate cloud on the curve of his now-bare pec.

He stared down at it, wearing that thunderstruck expression again. It only deepened when she swiped her finger under the chocolate and brought the daub to her mouth, where she sucked it away.

"Yum."

He looked up. "I can't believe you just did that."

She thought he looked pretty cute, half-naked and all indignant. Carlo was no longer bleak, no longer serious, no longer mired in memories.

"Oh, stop it. You're being a fuddy-duddy again. The stuff's not poisonous. Why, I remember watching you and your brothers filling your mouths with whipped cream when we were all kids."

"Oh, yeah? There's a good idea." A light entered his eyes and he grabbed the can out of her hands. Then he advanced on her.

Lucy shuffled back. Not too far, because she could see he was playing now, too.

"Open up, Goose."

The small of her back smacked the edge of the counter. "Now, Carlo…"

But she couldn't stop the delight bubbling inside of

her or the smile breaking over her lips. *He* was teasing now, and truly, she didn't think he'd really go through with it.

"Lucy, open up."

"Oh, fine." But instead she stuck her tongue out at him.

And quick as a snake he coated it with the chocolate cream.

Surprised, she started to laugh, but then it died as he choked out a sound, then swooped down to cover her lips with his.

They both groaned.

Blame it on the chocolate, or on the previous kitchen kisses, or on the days of unacknowledged foreplay that had kept the tension high in the McMillan & Milano offices, but this time it didn't feel like experimentation, temptation or punishment.

This time it felt like pure passion.

"Lucy," he said against her mouth, even as his hands found the bare skin beneath her shirt and slid up her back. "*Lucy.*"

"Don't," she said, her voice fierce. "Don't talk anymore. Just kiss me."

Maybe there were some advantages to being the youngest Sutton. Yes, it made her the family's favorite screwup, but it also made her, and she'd admit it, just the tiniest bit spoiled. Sometimes she just wanted what she wanted. Right now.

And right now she wanted Carlo Milano. Damn the consequences.

Chapter Seven

Lucy shivered as Carlo's hands slid from her back to cup her breasts. Her nipples tightened and desire darted like white heat down between her thighs. Her heartbeat started pounding in her ears and her skin felt too tight for her bones.

"Lucy, are you sure—"

She ground her mouth against Carlo's to stifle his doubts. *I want it. I want him. Now.*

And if she let him hesitate, she'd be left unsatisfied. Still needy. Lust unrequited.

Spurred by the thought, she grabbed the hem of her shirt and stripped it over her head. He stepped back, his hands at his sides, and she fumbled with the front clasp of her bra on her own.

His nostrils flared as her bra slid down her arms.

Looking down, she could see herself, swollen breasts, taut nipples, the way her jittery breaths made her belly tremble.

One of Carlo's tanned hands reached out and his forefinger lightly circled her areola. She gasped, her fingers curling into fists and her eyes closing tight. Carlo's touch teased her again, the circle slow and maddening.

Worrying.

A snail's pace would give him time to think.

Carlo already thought way too much.

She grabbed his hand and pushed it against her breast. His palm felt hard and hot and she stepped closer. "Kiss me," she demanded. "I want your mouth."

His laugh was soft. Deliberate. "So impatient."

She thumbed his hard nipple and leaned in to lick the other with the very tip of her tongue. His fingers closed over her aching breast. She pressed herself into the harder touch and another shiver racked her body.

Carlo's free hand chased the movement down her spine until he slid his fingers beneath the waistband of her jeans at the small of her back. The snap on the front pressed into her belly and Lucy ripped it open.

His breath hissed out as his hand slid lower to heat a cheek left bared by her thong. Her hips crowded closer to his and he pressed his erection against the give of her abdomen. His face lowered to her hair. "Lucy, we should—"

"Take this to the bedroom," she finished for him, closing her eyes at the delicious sensation of his palm caressing her naked bottom. They weren't playing the start-and-stop game, not this time. She opened her eyes and her gaze lifted to his. "And I mean it."

He laughed, that soft, amused laugh, as if her fierceness didn't frighten him. "Else what? You're going to bite me?"

A little smile played across her mouth. "Or else I'm *not* going to bite you." And then she did, she bit him, a tiny nip right into the hard muscle of his chest wall.

Carlo jerked, and then in a blink he had her in his arms and was striding out of the kitchen. Giddy with triumph, she clung to him as her blood sped around her body just like her brothers' slot cars used to careen around their zigzagging track. In a darkened bedroom, she only had the impression of austere space before she found herself dropped to a wide mattress.

Carlo stood beside it, looking down at her.

Her bare torso was pale in the shadows and in the vee of her unfastened jeans was a slice of the brighter white of her thong. Lucy toed off her shoes and socks, then went to work dragging off the clinging denim pants under his scrutinizing gaze.

She marveled at herself all the while. As much as she felt the need for speed, because giving Carlo time for second thoughts meant there'd be no follow-through for them, getting naked for a man wasn't the most natural of Lucy Sutton maneuvers. She'd had a few lovers—three—but at this stage of the process she'd always felt a little fear mixed with the want in the pit of her belly.

A man was so much bigger. So much stronger. So much...other.

But now, with Carlo…

She kicked her pants over the side of the bed and hooked a thumb in each side of her thong. With Carlo she felt only breathless anticipation.

"Stop right there," he ordered.

She froze. Her gaze jumped to his, but his eyes were impenetrable in the dark room. Just more shadows.

The bed dipped as his hip settled on the mattress. His hand cupped the vee between her thighs. "What's your hurry?"

Hot, liquid desire rushed to meet the warmth of his hand. "I…I…" There was a reason, but she couldn't remember right now what it was. "You…you…"

"Am the one who will be setting the pace." He leaned over to deliver an almost-chaste kiss to her mouth, her lips softened by the need his expert fingers were stoking. They rubbed lightly over the satiny fabric of her panties. "I'm the boss."

Her legs edged open and she reached for his shoulders to bring him closer. His chest brushed the tips of her breasts as he let her draw him down. "I've never been the best of employees, Mr. Milano." Her voice sounded strained, but what else could she do? If he wouldn't let her rush, then he had to let her keep it light.

Make it a game.

"So maybe you could outline the rules for me," she added.

"Hmm. All right." He straightened, going business-like. "Take a memo, Ms. Sutton."

Her fingers wandered over his nearest thigh to find his hard length behind his jeans. His hand caught her searching digits before they could curl around his erection.

"Ms. Sutton!" he said in mock shock.

"I'm only looking for a pencil," she protested.

He choked back his laugh, then directed her touch himself so that she located her target. It was gratifyingly thick. Even through denim he felt hot.

"Oh, Mr. Milano. This instrument may be a little larger than I'm used to."

His stern voice hid more laughter. "Are you bucking for a raise?" She heard him suck in a breath as she used the heel of her hand to trace his length. "Never mind then, Ms. Sutton, I'll write the memo myself."

She could have cried as his hand left its aching niche between her thighs, his forefinger drawing a line from the cleft upward, on the way bumping sensitive places that made her squirm against the spread.

"From Carlo Milano," he whispered into the dark around them as his finger made curlicues across her midriff. "To all temporary employees."

"*All* temporary employees?" she questioned.

His hand stilled. "Point taken. Thank you, Ms. Sutton. To all small, blond, sexy yet temporary secretaries named Lucy. When in bed, there's no rushing the tasks at hand. There's no taking shortcuts. Clothes are optional—" and here he drew her thong down himself "—and screaming in pleasure is completely necessary."

She should have laughed. It was a game after all, a seductive little game that she'd started. He was taking over, coming down on the mattress and between her legs so that they had to widen to accommodate him. He was still wearing his jeans, and the denim abraded the sensitive skin of her inner thighs as he leaned down to suck her nipple.

But the suction of his hot, wet mouth set aside everything in her mind except how right his weight felt, how well he knew to stoke her fire, how the way he blew air over her damp nipple was going to make her mad. "Carlo—"

"Mr. Milano," he corrected, moving over to her other breast.

She gasped as he drew it into his mouth. "Mr. Milano, that…that…oh, keep doing that."

What had she been thinking? She never wanted to hurry this part. And he kept his promise about setting the pace. The slow, slow pace. He left her breasts, left them aching, to move up her neck and explore the hollow behind her ears, the smooth skin at her temples, and to draw a line down her nose with the tip of his tongue.

She leaped like a fish to catch his mouth with hers and she heard him give another of those low laughs as he delivered nipping little kisses on her lips. But that wasn't what she wanted, she wanted more—long kisses, luscious kisses, tongue kisses. Her hands gripped his hair to hold him closer, but he grabbed her wrists and pressed them gently to the mattress.

"Patience, Ms. Sutton," he whispered against her ear, setting off another rush of goose bumps over her skin and liquid heat between her legs.

"Mr. Milano," she panted out, struggling against his hold, which did nothing more than twist their torsos together so that his crisp chest hair teased her aching breasts. "Mr. Milano, I…I think I have some messages I was supposed to deliver to you."

He reared up to look into her face, but again the shadows kept him in the dark. "What kind of messages?"

She raised up to kiss his stubbled chin. Wow. Even the whiskers turned her on. "Personal messages. Might I…I give them to you now?"

His hold loosened on her wrists and she took advantage of the moment to eel out from underneath him. Then she pushed him flat on the bed and leaned in to deliver the kiss she wanted. Long. Wet. Her tongue, she hoped, delivered the communication that she was really, really having a good time here.

His hands caressed her naked hips as she raised her head. She heard him swallow. "Interesting, Ms. Sutton. Are there…are there any others like that?"

"Like that and more." She leaned in to deliver them, even as her hand sneaked down his belly. His stomach muscles twitched and his hand closed more tightly on the curve of her hip as she found the placket of his jeans. Then they were loosened and her hand found the hard heat that was so silky smooth to her touch.

Carlo dispensed with his jeans and his briefs in the speediest move he'd yet to make. Finally he and Lucy were naked next to each other and exchanging all kinds of communiqués: smooth to muscled, hard to yielding, man to woman.

He rolled on a condom. Then her hips tilted to take him in and they both groaned as he slid inside her. The delicious pressure set her to squirming again, and he clamped his hand once more around her hip in an attempt to still her instinctive movements. "Baby…"

"That's *Ms.* Baby," she said, squeezing her eyes shut as he drew out again, the slick friction so sweet and hot that she wanted to beg for more.

"Ms. Baby, this is so damn good. What…what is your critique, if I may ask?"

"Thank you…thank you so much for your interest in my opinion, Mr. Milano. And I, too, think it's very, very good."

Then he started a driving rhythm that made speech, let alone games, impossible. To keep up, Lucy wrapped her thighs around his hips, but he was making her mindless. Release was rushing toward her and she didn't know whether to hold back or run toward its way.

Then Carlo slid his hand between their bodies and stroked the sweetest spot of all. "I think it's time, Ms. Sutton," he said. "I think it's time to scream."

After she did, after he came with an intensity that included a small, stinging bite on her shoulder, Carlo tucked Lucy into the bed beside him. They didn't talk. They didn't do anything to shatter the sated mood.

Sometime in the still-dark hours of the morning, she woke to find him at her breasts again—how quickly he'd learned her weakness! He drew her on top of him this time and she undulated against him, setting the pace, taking what she wanted, giving what he asked for in encouraging whispers.

They slept again.

The next time Lucy woke, the room was filled with

pale gray light. Carlo was on the other pillow, studying her face.

She instantly felt a chill at his somber expression. "We shouldn't have—" he started.

"Oh, no," she said, jerking instantly upright. She didn't even bother to hold the sheet against her breasts. "Oh, no, no, no."

"What?"

"Don't you go all fuddy-duddy on me now."

Annoyance replaced the seriousness on his face. "I wish you wouldn't use that term."

"I wish you wouldn't force me to." Now she drew up the sheet, even as she started edging out of the bed. "I'm not going to let you take all the fun out of this."

"The 'fun'?"

"Well, ye-ah." She frowned at him, as fierce as she could make it. "Have you forgotten the whipped cream? What would you call our little boss-secretary role playing, huh? Huh?"

"Lucy—"

"Look. I've got to get back to Elise's. Then I have this family brunch thing. So listen to me fast and listen to me good. Last night we were both in need of a little fun. So that's what we had. Nothing more and nothing less."

And with luck, she'd have to say nothing else about it. No matter *what* she might want to say. No matter when she figured out what exactly that might be.

Lucy carried a tray of orange juice onto the back patio and stopped before her father. "OJ, Dad?"

He took a glass and she moved on to one of her older brothers, Sam. His nose was buried in the business section of the Sunday paper and she raised her foot to tap the middle with her sandal. "Hey, Mr. Wall Street. Want something to drink?"

He looked up at her as he folded the paper into his lap. "Don't mind if I do. And what's got you all rosy-cheeked this a.m., Goose?"

Rosy cheeks went even redder under his scrutiny, if their heat was any indication. Lucy wasn't going to give him her first guess, though. Telling her brother she was suffering from beard burn was just not going to happen. "What's with the newspaper?" she said, changing the subject as she slid her tray onto a nearby end table. "Don't you get enough financial fodder with your weekday dose of the *Wall Street Journal?*"

He stretched out his long legs and ran a hand over his crisp, short golden hair. "I was poring over the want ads for you, little sister. Someone's got to be concerned about your future."

"For a minute there I thought she could make a mighty fine waitress, but then she neglected to bring *me* a glass of orange juice," Jason, her other brother, complained. "Thanks for nothing, Lucy."

She shook her head, looking between their handsome, supercilious faces. "And to think I moved back to San Diego because I missed you guys." Still, she carried over a juice to Jason, sprawled on a cushioned lounge chair.

"You came back because you were broke," he said, reaching for the glass.

At that, she lifted it higher, letting the liquid slosh over the rim of the glass. "Whoops," she said as juice spilled onto the lenses of his dark glasses. "Look what I just did."

He sprang to his feet as liquid ran toward his chin, whipping off his sunglasses and then lunging for her as she leaped away from him. "Lucy, you'll pay for that."

From her safe position behind her father's chair she grinned at him. "And how am I going to do that when you're so sure I'm broke?"

Her brother gave up and turned toward the hose coiled in a nearby corner. Water gushed out, and he rinsed his glasses and then filled his cupped palm with water to clean his face, too. He glanced over his shoulder, his gaze speculative, but Lucy hadn't moved from behind her father's chair. She laughed.

"Foiled again, Jase," she said, knowing that if he could have gotten a clear shot she'd be drenched by now.

Her mother came out just as he started making another threat for future retaliation. "And here I thought my children were all grown-up," she scolded, though Lucy could tell she was so happy to have them there that they could have started an all-out food fight and Laura Sutton wouldn't have minded. She was slender and as short as Lucy, and it was amazing to think she'd produced two six-foot-tall boys, not to mention Lucy and Elise.

Which reminded her...

"Where's Elise and John, Mom?" Everyone in the family knew about Germaine McMillan's fall, and Lucy had adjusted the timeline a bit to cover her absence from her own bed at her sister's house. As far as the Sutton family members knew, she'd spent all of the night before at the hospital, not just part of it. When she'd made it back to Elise's that morning, her sister and John had already left to run a 10K, but they were expected to arrive for the brunch.

"Your sister and brother-in-law are stuck in traffic." Lucy's mother settled one hip on the arm of Lucy's dad's chair, and he automatically settled his hand on her thigh. "What's going on out here?" she asked.

Sam spoke up. "I was going through the want ads to find Lucy a job."

Lucy's mouth tightened. "I *have* a job."

"Well, and how's that going?" he went on. "You haven't said."

Four pairs of Sutton eyes turned on her. Lucy cleared her throat. "Fine."

"Are you showing up on time? Taking a normal lunch hour?"

Lucy bristled at her brother's interrogation. "Work days start at eleven, right? And lunch goes from twelve-thirty to three?"

"Lucy…" her mother started. "We love you. Your brother is just trying to—"

"Imply I'm lazy? Suggest I don't know how to be an employee?"

"Goose, come on." To his credit, Sam appeared sincere. "You have to admit it's a bit…strange that you couldn't stick with any of those jobs in Phoenix."

"Strange for the Suttons. But a lot of other people

find that their first position out of college isn't exactly right."

"Or, in your case, the second, and then the third?" This was from Jason. Leave it to a lawyer to trot out the facts.

"I worked plenty hard at those jobs and the people I worked for liked me." She just hadn't liked what she was doing for them. "I know you guys find that difficult to believe."

"Lucy." Her dad, the quietest of the bunch, entered the conversation. "Nobody's doubting your ability to do a good job."

"Remember all the work she did on her high school's prom?" her mom chimed in. "The principal gave her special recognition at the graduation ceremony. And then there were those very successful fund-raisers she spearheaded for her college sorority's charity."

"Thanks, Mom," Lucy replied. She *had* been damn good at organizing those events, just as she'd done well with things like the balloon festival postcollege. Of course, none of that impressed her siblings, who measured success by climbing rungs on the corporate ladder. "And I'm going to find the right place for me in San Diego. I will."

"Carlo will surely give you a good recommendation," Sam said. "That will help."

Lucy still didn't want to talk about Carlo. She didn't want to think about him, about last night, about how his touch had set her on fire. Thank goodness it was Sunday and she had time away from him to forget that sexy laugh in his voice—would she ever hear "Ms. Sutton" again and not want to quiver?—and the seriously sensual way they'd come together the second time, his palms dragging over her skin and igniting fires in every cell.

"He *will* give you a good recommendation, right, Lucy?"

"What?" she looked around, surprised to find herself out on her parents' patio when she'd been so lost in her memories a second before. "Who?"

Sam rolled his eyes. "What exactly are you doing at McMillan & Milano, anyway? Given the way you're so distracted I hope it's nothing that requires more concentration than opening envelopes."

"Samuel!" her mother scolded. "If that's your way of encouraging your sister…"

He waved off the criticism. "Goose knows I only want the best for her. But I'm concerned, Mom. We're all concerned." He sighed. "Goose, I'm sorry if I seem like I'm coming down hard on you. That's not my intention."

"I know." Lucy sighed, too. This was the curse of being the youngest sibling. Your family remembered you as the five-year-old who couldn't spell, and then it didn't help that you didn't grow up and instantly become a corporate clone of the rest of them. She knew they loved her. She loved their hypersuccessful, hyperjudgmental selves right back.

She only wished they'd trust her to find her own way to her own kind of success. Wherever that was. Whatever that was. She eyed the newspaper her brother had cast aside and then crossed over to pick it up. Accounting positions started on page P-2.

The fine print swam before her eyes and she closed them, picturing herself spending the next thirty years inside the black-and-gray world of a classified ad. Orderly, colorless, one column after another after another after another. Just like accounting. Why had she studied it anyhow? Because her family thought it was a good idea.

Bleh. But she forced her attention to return to the pages. "There's probably a position just made for me in here," she said, her voice bright. "I graduated with honors. I have accounting experience in different types of businesses."

"Good spin, sis. Better than 'I've changed jobs as often as some people change hairstyles.'"

She ignored her attorney brother's latest attack.

"How much longer will you be working for Carlo?" her mom asked.

Oh, that name had to come up again. Lucy left the dreary world of black-and-white and set sail on yet more memories. Swallowing a snicker, she remembered Carlo's surprise when she'd sprayed him with the chocolate whipped cream. Wouldn't that be fun to try again? Next time, she wouldn't use her finger to clean his naked skin of the fluffy stuff. Next time, it would be her tongue, and she could well imagine his little jerk of reaction as she stroked it across his bare pectoral…

But there wouldn't be a next time, right?

Or *could* there be a next time?

Aaargh. In bed that morning, Lucy had been worried about *his* reaction to last night. Now she saw that she should have been worrying about her own, too. What did she want to happen next?

She didn't know what she wanted to happen next. That's why she'd cut off the discussion this morning. She'd insisted to him it was all in fun, but was it a *single* night of fun? Is that what he wanted? Is that what *she* wanted? She couldn't think beyond those memories of his deep kisses and his tender touch.

Ms. Sutton, I think it's time to scream.

"Earth to Goose. Earth to Goose."

Lucy swam free of the latest wave of remembered longing to hear her brother's pestering voice. Lowering the newspaper, she frowned at him. "What now?" She didn't want to come back to earth. Putting her feet on the ground meant coming to terms with the new situation with Carlo.

And she was so confused about that.

She noticed the whole family was staring at her again. "What? *What?*"

Jason looked over at Sam. "I didn't think it was possible, but she's become goosier than ever. I don't think she's heard a word we've been saying."

"About what?" Lucy demanded.

"About what you're doing at McMillan & Milano. Dad got wind that you've taken over some project involving the Street Beat festival. Is that a good idea?"

"What do you mean?"

"I don't know," Jason answered. "But you're trained as an accountant. Should you be involving yourself with a *music* festival? I've heard about Claudia Cox and word has it she's not known for her patience or her generosity. You don't want to screw up the job when it's Carlo who will pay the price."

Lucy's insecurities slithered out of the holes in her psyche like eels from coral-reef caves. She was trained as an accountant and had never loved her duties in that kind of work—even though she was good at it. Why did she presume that her Street Beat responsibilities would go smoothly? She was an accountant. A numbers person.

"Maybe…maybe you're right," she heard herself say. "Carlo…" The festival wasn't something to take lightly. It was his work, his reputation, his business. What if she did screw up? She licked her lips. "Carlo…"

And then it was Carlo's own voice that finished the sentence she was trying to form. "Is very satisfied with everything Lucy's done."

Chapter Eight

There was a flurry of greetings as Carlo joined them on the patio. He glanced over at Lucy. "Your mother called a little bit ago and invited me over for brunch," he said, replying to the surprise that was surely written all over her face. "I guess she forgot to tell you. I caught a ride with Elise and John. Maybe you'll give me a lift to my car later?"

"Oh. Um, sure." Of course. They'd left his Lexus yesterday at the office when she'd driven them to the beach. Had that only been yesterday that they'd been at the beach, and then at the hospital, and then in his bed? Her gaze skittered away from his.

Don't make a fool of yourself, Lucy. But it wasn't easy facing him for the first time in front of her family. If her cheeks had been red before, they had to be glowing scarlet now, and she didn't want anyone guessing there was anything romantic going on between the two of them.

Because of course there wasn't.

Last night had just been…

Fun. *She'd* labeled it that, not him, and she refused to make more of it now. And it was *private* fun, so she had to get it together or one of her nosy siblings was bound to figure out something was up and embarrass the heck out of her over it.

Or worse, embarrass Carlo.

She managed to look him in the eye. "Do you know how Germaine is doing this morning?"

"Very well. Dot's already taken her home. I'll visit this afternoon."

"Which means you have plenty of time now to tell us everything, Carlo," Sam called out. "We can't count on Goose to give us the real skinny when it comes to her employment adventures. How's our Ms. Sutton handling her job responsibilities?"

Ms. Sutton.

Lucy's gaze jumped to Carlo again, she couldn't help herself. He was studying his glass of OJ, but as if he felt her looking at him, he lifted his tangle of dark lashes and stared right back.

Ms. Sutton, it's time to scream.

"Carlo?" Sam prodded. "I swear, you're as distracted as Lucy's been all morning. If I didn't know better—"

They were spared the end of that sentence by the arrival of Elise and John, who'd been delayed in the kitchen by a coffee ring they'd brought and had cut into wedges. Now they were ready to pass the pieces around.

"Sweets?" Elise smiled up at Carlo as she offered him a plate. He smiled back down at her and it struck Lucy, for the millionth time in her life, how perfect her sister was with her smooth, Grace Kelly hair, her long legs, her slender figure—she'd already run a 10K that morning! Add to that the fact that she'd recently received yet another big promotion at work.

It wasn't Elise's fault that males had always been drawn to her, despite her unswerving devotion to her husband. Who wouldn't be attracted to such loveliness?

And at the moment, Carlo looked as if he couldn't pull his gaze away from her. Lucy wished it didn't make her feel so stupid and glum. Not to mention short.

A plate of the strudel-y pastry didn't make her lousy mood go away. It just made her feel more dowdy than ever. Neither did her sister's sharp look. "What's the matter, Luce?" she said, keeping her voice below the rest of the conversation on the patio.

Lucy kept her gaze wide-eyed and innocent. "Not a thing. Why do you ask?"

Elise frowned. "You—"

Jason's loud voice drowned out her sister's next remark. "C'mon, Carlo. You've had orange juice, you've had pastry, and Mom's famous egg-and-potato bake is on its way. It's only fair you provide a little entertainment."

"Gee, Jase," he answered. "I left my accordion at home. Maybe you can play us a tune on your harmonica."

"Funny," her brother said. "But I just told you what I'm looking for. Give us the dirt on our Goose. Surely she's done something lately to liven up your days."

Lucy felt her face freeze. *His days...and his nights.*

"Yeah," her other brother chimed in. "We can never figure out why she's played musical desk chairs—"

"Three companies in as many years, Sam," Lucy heard herself protest. "It's not as if..."

But she broke off on a sigh. The way the other Sutton siblings were looking at her she knew that to them, three different jobs in such a short time might as well be thirteen. They just could not comprehend that someone in their family wouldn't land in their dream position after graduation and then succeed beyond everyone's wildest expectations.

"Never mind," she muttered, looking away from them. "You guys won't understand."

Nor would they let up. Maybe if their parents hadn't gone off to the kitchen with Elise's John to put the finishing touches on brunch, her brothers would have abandoned the subject. But they were still looking to have fun at her expense. Hard to believe they were over thirty.

They turned back to her boss. "Tell us how she does it," Sam insisted. "How does she sabotage all her employment opportunities? Does she spill coffee over her keyboard? Take pictures of her naked butt on the copy machine? Sharpen the pens instead of the pencils?"

How many times had she told them she'd never been fired? They never believed her. Lucy jammed her hands in the pockets of her jeans and pretended to ignore their conversation by inspecting a hibiscus bush on the edge of the patio. But the long silence coming from Carlo had her turning to take a peek at him.

He was frowning at her brothers. "You two make me want to call my little sister Franny."

Her male siblings exchanged glances. "Huh?"

"I think I need to drop to my knees for some serious groveling in case I've ever been even half as obnoxious to her as you are to Lucy."

Sam sat straighter in his chair, his expression shocked. "Wait a sec—"

"We're not obnoxious to Goose," her other brother interrupted. "We care about Goose. Who told her that her front tire needed air?"

"I leant her forty bucks two weeks ago."

"Which I paid back to you the next day," Lucy said through her teeth. "The ATM was broken."

If her brothers hadn't looked so honestly bewildered, she might have been angrier at them. If she didn't know they'd take a bullet for her and didn't see how their teasing got so out of hand, she might have given them a dose of their own medicine. As it was, she just wanted to knock their two blockheads together and call it a day.

"Anyway, what does that have to do with shedding light on Lucy and her work habits?" Really, she supposed by definition a lawyer was tenacious, but Jason was the type who never let go of anything. "My bet's on the naked-butt copying."

Carlo shook his head. "There's been *no* naked—" He broke off, cleared his throat, started again. "She's done absolutely nothing like what you're talking about."

"You don't have to cover for her. We love the little screwup just as she is." Sam beamed a smile full of that emotion at her even as she shook her head. Cripes. Nothing like ruining her image around her boss. Apparently they'd known Carlo for too long to even think of that.

Carlo's arms crossed over his chest. "You guys are unbelievable. I'm not covering anything. As a matter of fact, Lucy's an exemplary employee. Besides all the regular secretarial duties she stepped in to perform so ably, she's impressed the hell out of one of my clients and has taken on an additional project of her own for *Street Beat.* So you two had better lay off Lucy or I'll be forced to remind you what my fist feels like against your faces. We might have been twelve the last time we went a round or two, but I assure you I'm in better shape now."

Sam and Jason stared at Carlo, dumbfounded again and this time completely shaken from their descent into adolescence. Elise murmured, "That's the longest speech I've heard him make in the past six years." Another heartbeat passed, then the three Sutton siblings turned as one to look at Lucy, something that looked dangerously like speculation sparkling in their eyes.

Uh-oh. Though half of her wanted to dissolve in tears and the other half wanted to kiss Carlo silly in gratitude for his support, the suspicion on her brothers' and sister's faces called for something else entirely. There was no way she wanted them to figure out there was anything more than employer-to-employee respect between herself and the dark-haired man on the patio.

So she did what she could to draw them off the scent.

Throwing up her hands, she ran over to her temporary boss and flung herself against his chest. "My hero!" she cried out dramatically. His arms automatically closed around her back, making her want to cry even more.

What a sap she was. But she couldn't, just couldn't, let him or anyone else know how much his defense meant to her. Then they might make assumptions about how much *he* meant to her. So instead, she made a big play of looking over her shoulder at Jason. "Can I borrow that forty again?"

Puzzled, he drew out his wallet. "Sure."

She stuffed the two bills into Carlo's breast pocket. "Like I said, fella, there's more where that came from anytime you can get these two arrogant juvenile idiots off my back." With a big wink, she sashayed out of his embrace.

The Lucy Show seemed to satisfy her brothers—after another moment they laughed at her like she'd hoped they would. Then the conversation moved on to sports and Lucy was able to retreat to her hibiscus bush again.

She blew out a long breath. That had been close. One of the very reasons Carlo had not wanted to give in to their mutual attraction was because it would make events like this awkward. So it definitely would have been a disaster if this morning-after was marred by her family's intrusion into what she and Carlo hadn't figured out yet for themselves.

Fun, Lucy, she reminded herself. *You did figure it out, or at least you told him you did. You told him it was a night of fun and not to make any more of it than that.*

It *wasn't* any more than that.

Still, she wanted to keep the events of the previous night private.

"Lucy!" Her sister hissed her name.

She gave a guilty start and turned to face Elise. "What?" On the other side of the patio, the men were still talking among themselves. "What's the matter?"

"You're the matter," Elise said, her voice almost a whisper. "I know where you were last night."

"I told you. At the hospital, and when I called I also told you that I didn't know if I'd make it home before morning." All true.

"Don't give me that." Elise slid a glance over her shoulder, then pinned Lucy with her gaze. "You were with Carlo."

"Of course. I told you. We were together when the call came about Germaine—"

"You were with Carlo and you and he had sex."

The last word gave Lucy another guilty start. "I don't know why you think—"

"It's written all over your face, and Lucy, he's going to break your heart."

She swallowed. "My heart's not involved. It was just…just…for fun."

Her sister rolled her eyes.

It was just…just…for fun. Had she really said that? Now it sounded stupid to her own ears. Who had sex with a long-time family friend for *fun?*

"Lucy, how could you be so foolish? He's not interested in anything long-term. You're going to have to get that through your head."

Lucy's heart fell like a stone to the pit of her stomach. Her sister was right. Carlo wasn't interested in anything long-term because Elise, the love of his life, was standing right in front of her.

Gazing at her sister's lovely face, she thought of why he'd looked so sadly at Lucy this morning. She'd known how he felt about Elise. And in the light of day, he'd probably regretted waking up in bed with the shorter, bubbly-yet-bumbling version of the woman he'd always pine for.

If Carlo had expected to find the drive from the Sutton family home to the McMillan & Milano offices uncomfortable, he was quickly proved wrong. After squeezing into the passenger seat of Lucy's car, he had to do nothing more than listen while she pattered about some story her father had told them over brunch.

It was natural. Easy. As if everything between them was fine. Unchanged.

He rubbed his palms against his thighs and tried to find a few more inches for his long legs. Wasn't this every single man's dream come true? A spectacular night in the sack without any resulting changes in the status quo.

Yeah. Every single man's dream, and since Lucy herself had proposed it would go like this—that it was nothing more and nothing less than "fun"—then he had no reason to do anything but sit back and breathe through it.

Still, when she paused, he figured it was only fair he do his part in keeping the easy conversation going.

"What do you have planned for the rest of your day off?" he asked.

Her sweet mouth turned up at the corners in a little smile. "If you must know, Mr. Milano..."

Mr. Milano. The words fell like the clunk of the other shoe into the middle of the car's sudden quiet.

Mr. Milano. A dozen images bombarded Carlo's brain. Lucy, naked and stretched out before him, the pale curves of her breasts topped by nipples he'd made hard and wet with his mouth. Her slender wrists held gently in one of his hands as she squirmed against his mattress. The perfect, glistening shell-pink flesh he'd discovered between her thighs.

He barely held back his groan. "Lucy...Lucy, about last night—"

"Please. Let's not talk about it."

"Are you blushing?" Believe it or not, a flush was definitely crawling up her neck to her cheeks. He stared. "Wasn't it you who broke out the chocolate whipped cream?"

She licked her bottom lip. "It was the heat of the moment."

"It was hot, all right."

"It was *fun.*"

"Lucy..."

He saw her fingers tighten on the steering wheel. "What's wrong with fun? Where in the male-female relations manual does it say sex has to be performed with a proper level of gravitas?"

"Nowhere." He sighed. But he didn't want her to think that it made what they'd done together meaningless or forgettable. He didn't want to be yet another man in her life, like her brothers Jason and Sam, who didn't take her seriously.

Lucy, for all her sunshiny nature, deserved better. Or maybe *because* of her sunshiny nature, she deserved his best.

She deserved his honesty. Though she'd given him that perfect excuse for ducking from it—"let's not talk about it," she'd just said—he didn't need to go along.

"Lucy, would you mind driving me to the hospital before going to get my car?"

For the first time since they'd climbed into the Volkswagen, she darted a look at him. "I don't know…"

The Suttons were all so damn smart. She could tell he had his own agenda and wasn't sure she wanted to comply. "Please," he said.

She shot him another look, gave a little shrug, then changed lanes and took the appropriate exit. He didn't continue until she'd pulled into a spot in the hospital's visitors' parking lot.

Though the sights and smells of the hospital corridors couldn't reach him here, Carlo's gut was already knotting. He wiped a hand down his face and reminded himself that he owed Lucy an explanation. She'd been there for him last night when he needed someone and there was no reason not to share this with her. He'd stay calm and cool and the whole conversation would soon be over.

Then he would have done the right thing and then they could go forward, because he would have assuaged some of his guilt.

One hand swiped over his face yet again and he

finally started, trying to ignore the gruffness in his voice. "I need to tell you about how I was feeling last night. About why we ended up in bed when I was so certain we shouldn't before."

"I know why you've been resisting," Lucy said quickly. She was staring out the windshield and her hands were still on the steering wheel, as if she was planning a quick getaway.

He frowned at her. "You know?"

She spoke the next words with the same speed one ripped a bandage off a wound. "It's because of Elise."

"What?" Astonishment cracked his voice.

Lucy continued staring out the windshield. "I've known about it for years. Since her wedding day. You're in love with Elise."

"Good God." He tilted his head to stare at the Volks-wagen's roof. "Where to start? Believe me, Lucy, last night…at no point did any of that concern Elise."

"Okay."

It was not an okay-I-believe-you kind of an okay, but an okay-I'll-humor-you okay. "Lucy, I'm not in love with Elise!"

Lucy remained silent.

He shook his head. "Do I strike you as the kind of man who would torture myself over the past six years by hanging around with my best friend if I was in love with his wife?"

"You don't hang around so much anymore, not ac-cording to my sister."

He grimaced. "Don't tell me Elise thinks I'm in love with her. I don't believe that for a minute."

"She just noted that you're kind of…remote these days. You know, arrive late to social gatherings, leave early…."

"I get it. I'm not the life of the party anymore."

"I thought I understood why," Lucy said quietly. "I thought I understood why you gravitated toward the distant corner. I thought I saw something, heard something at Elise and John's wedding…"

He shook his head. There she went again. Lucy saw things about him that no one else ever knew. "You're wrong about how I feel now. Okay, on Elise and John's wedding day…which was a *long* time ago, I did experience a brief pang. But it was brief and then it was eclipsed by…"

He sighed, even at the hospital it was hard to push out the words. Settling for others, he said, "I was never what you'd call a party animal, Luce—"

"You used to laugh, though. And you used to make up limericks. Not dirty ones, just…funny ones. You had a new one every time I saw you."

He'd forgotten about that. It seemed forever ago, but the memory made him smile. "You know what? I collected those for you, Lucy."

"Me?"

"You're the only person in the world who knows I used to have a limerick side."

"So what happened?" Lucy asked. "Where did all the limericks go?"

Hesitating, he gazed out the side window.

"If it's not Elise, then it's Pat. It's about your partner's death."

His head whipped toward her. "What makes you

think that?" He thought he was so careful to keep its effect hidden from everyone.

"I was with you at the hospital, remember? And then that night at Germaine's, too. The night of the Street Beat party."

The night she'd seen how weak the memories had made him. The night she'd stepped in and distracted him from the way they seemed to suck him down.

"Last night…last night you did for me what you did that other time, Lucy. Sometimes…sometimes remembering gets to be too much."

"Do you want to tell me about what happened?"

Carlo inhaled a breath. It was why he'd come here, yet still he hesitated.

"He was shot, right?"

Shot. Four letters. One word. It had all happened that simply and that quickly. "We were heading back from an interview. Saw a patrol car with a lone cop who'd pulled over a van full of teenagers in a residential area of working-class homes."

It had rained earlier. The wipers on their unmarked detective's vehicle had left a sludge of mud in the corners of their windshield, and the smell of wet asphalt filled the car when Pat unrolled his window to check if the police officer wanted help with his traffic stop.

Yes, he'd appreciate it. There was a passel of kids who were milling on the sidewalk and they were distracting the officer from his job.

"Pat got out to keep a lid on the kids, but first he strapped into his bulletproof vest. Just a precaution as there had been some gang activity in the area. I drove up the street to find a place to pull over. I put on my own vest, then I was getting out of the car when I heard gunshots."

He'd dived back in the car and grabbed the radio to call for assistance. Then he'd peered over the seat and saw that everyone on the scene, from the patrol cop to the smallest of the teenagers, had gone belly-down. He'd crept out of the car, staying low with his gun in hand, and he'd barked at them, ordering them not to move.

Almost immediately more police appeared on the scene and surrounded the kids. The bullets hadn't come from them, but from someplace across the street, Carlo had figured. When there weren't any further gunshots, the kids started to stir. And that's when Carlo realized Pat wasn't moving at all.

"The bullet pierced him under the armhole of his vest. Unlucky shot, I guess." The end of a life.

Carlo stared out the windshield, remembering Pat's drenched sleeve, the last glimmers of awareness in his eyes, the bewildered look on Germaine's face when Carlo had broken the news. His hands had still been sticky with his partner's blood.

Now he locked down on his memories, refusing to let them run free. His emotions, too, he locked away.

"He was six weeks away from retirement. Germaine couldn't comprehend how it had happened." Carlo had watched, helpless, as she fell apart. "She's stronger now," he said, "but then…but then… I did the best I could. I made the funeral arrangements. I went through his closet and drawers." Even though each time he touched an article of Pat's clothing, Carlo could still see the blood on his hands.

"I'm sorry," Lucy whispered.

"Last night…last night I remembered it all too well."

"Carlo…" He heard her sniff.

He lifted his gaze to her face. "Oh, Lucy." She was crying, the tears flowing down her cheeks. "I didn't tell you this to upset you."

"I know. But I know how you must feel—"

"That's the thing, Luce. That's how I'm different now. I usually don't feel. Not too much."

"What?"

"I work. I work some more. I think about work. I try not to think about anything else or get too caught up in the past or with other people. I like it that way."

"Carlo…"

"It's how I want it, Lucy. It's why I don't do the couple thing, it's why I shouldn't be here right now, raining on all your bright sunshine. I like my distance. I like my darkness. I'm most comfortable without strong connections. It's why I'm better off alone in those distant corners."

She nodded. Drying her cheeks with the backs of her hands, she appeared to understand and accept his explanation. It was all true, anyway, and he should be feeling better for it, except…

Except Carlo suddenly couldn't shake the notion that Lucy's tears would be as hard to forget as the sight of his partner's blood.

Chapter Nine

Lucy straightened a small memo pad on the seat of an empty chair and arranged a sharpened pencil at a perpendicular angle beside it. She'd pushed back the partition between the two conference rooms in the McMillan & Milano offices so that all fifty volunteers for the Street Beat festival could be seated during their one and only orientation meeting, scheduled for five-thirty that evening. Checking her watch, she felt her stomach give a nervous twitch, even though she'd checked and double-checked the arrangements.

There was a lot riding on this project. Of course, the high school students and parents needed to walk away from their volunteer experience with positive feelings about Street Beat, as well as McMillan & Milano. But there was more. Her temporary position at the security firm was coming to an end after this weekend—and she needed to walk away from it with something, too.

Sunday brunch at her parents the weekend before had made clear that she still had a long way to go in proving to her family that Lucy Goosey had grown up. She hoped a successful end to her Street Beat project would shut the traps of her confidence-crushing big brothers. And maybe a successful end to her employment at McMillan & Milano would take that look of concern out of Elise's eyes, too.

For days, her sister had been closely watching, as if expecting that at any minute Lucy would break down and fall apart over Carlo.

Wasn't going to happen. Learning that he didn't love Elise had been a surprise. Okay, a welcome surprise, but discovering how deeply he'd been affected by his partner's death made him as big a mistake for her as ever. Sure, he didn't love her sister, but she was just as sure he didn't want to love any other woman, either.

So she'd rededicated herself to the job and to demonstrating to everyone—maybe most of all herself— that Lucy Sutton was on the path to success in her life. No more job failures, and certainly no more fixations on the completely wrong man.

Tonight's meeting was going to be the harbinger of the new, positive direction in her life.

"Wow," a voice said from the doorway.

Lucy jumped. Carlo. She darted a glance at him and went back to straightening the already-straight materials on the chair in front of her. She hadn't seen him much over the past few days, and she'd been grateful for that. He'd been busy at the Street Beat site and most of their contact had been in brief phone calls and the occasional text message.

"I like the visual aids," he said. At the front of the combined conference rooms she'd erected an easel. An enlarged map of the festival grounds sat upon it. Along with pads and pencils, she was putting a hand-size version of the same map on each of the seats. "It looks as if you have everything covered."

"Believe it or not," she replied, moving to another chair, "I've been trained to pay attention to details."

"Oh, Ms. Sutton, I know not to underestimate you."

Ms. Sutton. The two words froze her.

They really, really needed to stop slipping those Ms. Suttons and Mr. Milanos into conversation. She supposed he hadn't meant to do it any more than she had, but still, when he used that name...

She darted another glance at him. He was leaning against the doorjamb in shirtsleeves and loosened tie. His hair was mussed, as if he'd been running his hands through it, and stubble darkened the angular line of his jaw.

Ms. Sutton. It echoed in her mind, and in a blink, her attention jumped back to that night in his bed. His beard had been in evidence then, too, and her skin prickled, remembering the burn of those whiskers against her neck and between her bare breasts.

A strangled little moan escaped her tight throat. Her knees buckled and she tried hiding the reaction by sliding into one of the empty chairs, a handful of memo pads clutched against her chest.

"Lucy?" Carlo crossed toward her. "What's wrong?"

She held up a hand, hoping to keep him away. The last thing she needed was him distracting her before she had to face her fifty volunteers. "Nothing, nothing. Just, um, nothing."

Wearing a frown, he crossed to a table she'd set against one wall and grabbed one of the bottles of water she'd set out. He twisted off the top and handed it to her as he settled into the chair next to hers.

She closed her eyes, but that didn't help much. From here she could smell him, spicy and male, a scent that she remembered from the night in his bed, too. When she'd showered the next morning, that scent had risen off her skin to mingle with the steam.

"What's wrong?" His hand settled on her back.

She jerked away from his touch. "Don't!"

His eyebrows rose. "Lucy—"

"Sorry." She gripped the bottle. "I'm, um… I'm just a little edgy about tonight."

He gazed around the room. "You've crossed all the t's and dotted all the i's, Luce. There's nothing to be edgy about."

"Uh-uh." She jumped up to put more distance between them. "It's going to be fine."

"It had better be," said a new voice from the doorway.

Lucy swallowed her groan as the faint scent of Chanel No. 5 reached her nose. Claudia Cox. She posed in the doorway as if she were in an ad for designer wear: tall, thin and wearing her faintly superior smile.

With a wave of her hand, Lucy acknowledged the other woman. "I didn't expect to see you here."

Claudia strode into the conference room as if it were a fashion runway. "It's not that I don't have complete faith in your abilities but…"

I have no faith in your abilities, Lucy finished for her. Her stomach gave another little twist and she wondered if the office first aid kit included antacid tablets.

It's only fifty volunteers, she reminded herself.

Fifty volunteers.

And McMillan & Milano's reputation.

And pleasing Claudia Cox, the bloodthirsty huntress in charge of the Street Beat festival.

The bloodthirsty huntress was striding toward Lucy at this moment, as if she scented fresh prey. She halted in front of her and looked down from the advantage of her fashion-model-plus-four-inch-heels height. Her gaze traveled the length of Lucy's body and then back up. "She lives," Claudia pronounced.

Despite her nerves, Lucy laughed. Yeah, she wasn't wearing the funereal gear she'd had on the day she visited the concert promoter's offices. Though she watched Elise head off each morning looking elegant and polished in her tailored-to-the-nines suits, Lucy had decided against going that route any longer herself. It just did not suit—no pun intended. Instead she was wearing a silk dress that she'd paired with pumps that picked up the emerald-green in the wild paisley print.

It was bright, sure.

But it would keep the attention focused on her during the meeting.

And it felt like something Lucy Sutton would wear. Not a corporate clone.

Still, the way Claudia was appraising her through narrowed eyes made her slide a jittery hand down the dress. "Is...is everything all right?"

Claudia tapped a glossy nail against her red lips. "Wrench—you remember Wrench?"

"The singer for Silver Bucket. Of course I remember him." At first it had been thrilling to meet the lead of a band she loved, but quickly she'd determined he fit the egotistical, selfish stereotype. Five minutes in his company and she'd known she wasn't the least interested in playing groupie to his hot rocker.

"He mentioned another band to me...the Killer Angels. Do you know them?"

Okay, so he was a hot rocker with good indie-band tastes. Lucy nodded. "I found them through their Web site and then bought their last CD. All girls, though their lead singer has a bluesy, smoky voice that can go rocker hard or crooner soft. I think they've played some small clubs in L.A."

"I have a last-minute cancellation for the festival, and I'm looking to fill the spot. It's not prime time, but they've got to be able to hold the interest of a big crowd."

Lucy considered. "There's a nice mix on the CD I have. A couple of ballads, as well as some with a dance beat. And the band has a look. Kind of a hard-edged innocence. If I had a vote, they'd have mine."

"If you had a vote..." Claudia murmured, her eyes narrowing again. Then she pulled her cell phone from the slender leather portfolio she carried under her arm. "The Killer Angels it is."

But instead of making her call, she paused and slid

a look over at Carlo, still standing on the other side of the room. Her gaze came back to Lucy's face. "Wrench asked about you, by the way."

"Me?"

"Something about maybe getting together with you to party after their gig this weekend."

"I—"

"She's not going to 'party' with that guy," Carlo interjected. He strode over to join them. "I don't know where the hell he'd get the idea that Lucy's interested in him."

Lucy tried again. "I—"

"It's Wrench that's interested in Lucy, obviously," Claudia responded in a cool voice. "And I'm just passing the info along. No need to shoot the messenger, Carlo."

He slid a proprietary hand beneath the hair at Lucy's nape. "You can't blame a man for keeping his eye on the prize, Claudia." His palm caressed the tender skin of Lucy's neck and she locked her knees so they wouldn't betray her by buckling again.

"So that's the way it is? Still?" Claudia asked, one of her perfectly arched brows arching higher. "I thought maybe that had run its course."

Lucy couldn't stop herself from turning her head to raise her own brow in Carlo's direction. He was playing that "I have a girlfriend" game for Claudia, and it didn't seem right that a man who wanted to keep his distance from Lucy would use her to keep his distance from another woman. And maybe she did want to party with Wrench! Well, not really, but it wasn't up to him to decide how the "prize" wanted to conduct her social life.

Perhaps he could read all that on her face.

"Luce…" he said softly.

She let her second brow rise. "What?"

Two of his fingers caressed the side of her neck. "Luce. I don't… You can't…" He huffed out a sigh, followed it up with an "oh, hell," and then startled the breath out of her by lowering his mouth.

And kissing her in front of the huntress, the visual aids and fifty empty chairs.

They might as well have been filled with people, for all the attention she paid to them. Thoughts flew around her head.

No…

Why…

Why can't I pull away?

She sensed Claudia drawing back, but Lucy's eyes were closed and Carlo's mouth was so gentle yet so hot that a quiver tickled down her spine. She never wanted it to end, no matter who was there to witness it, no matter what else was supposed to be taking place—

Her eyes popped open and she shoved him away.

"My meeting," she said, wiping the back of her hand against her mouth. Thank God for that smudge-proof lipstick. "The volunteers should be here…"

Lucy checked her watch. Something inside her froze and her voice squeezed out in a tight whisper. "The volunteers should have been here twenty minutes ago."

Twenty minutes ago had been the scheduled start of her all-important meeting. The harbinger of her future.

Except there was no one there to attend.

* * *

Lucy's sudden, stricken expression yanked at Carlo's heart. "Honey." He moved forward to take her in his arms again, but she backed off.

Right. Okay. He wasn't supposed to be touching her—or, good grief, *kissing* her—anyway. So he shoved his hands in his pockets and pretended he didn't continue to feel the imprint of her mouth on his. Clearing his throat, he took another step back. "I'm sure they'll be here soon."

Lucy's gaze darted back to her watch. "It's 5:52, right?" she whispered, her voice strained. She shifted to give Claudia, still on the phone a few feet away, more of her back. "I don't have the wrong time, do I?"

"Lucy—"

"Check your watch!"

He turned his wrist. "It 5:53."

Her face paled. "That's p.m.? I didn't somehow get the day and night mixed up?"

He shook his head and couldn't help but smile a little. One kiss of hers could turn his world upside-down, too.

"No smiling!" she hissed. "This isn't funny."

To his shock, her eyes started to fill with tears. "Lucy." He reached for her again, remembered he shouldn't and let his hand drop.

"I messed up. Somehow I did something wrong. The wrong day, the wrong time, the wrong directions." She was blinking rapidly to prevent a spillover. "Oh, God, Jason and Sam are right. I *am* a perennial failure."

"Lucy—"

"I *always* get it wrong."

"Don't you think you're overreacting? The volunteers are probably delayed."

But she wasn't listening to a word he said. "I've got to think." Her hands clapped against the sides of her head. "I've got to figure out a way to fix this."

She rushed out of the conference room.

Claudia looked up from her phone call and met Carlo's gaze. *Is she okay?* she mouthed.

"Perfectly fine," Carlo assured the other woman. *Make that perfectly nuts,* he thought. But she was his perfectly nutty responsibility, so he headed after her. What had set her off? Had it…had it been his kiss?

Yeah, right. Though the kiss had affected him, once again obliterating all his good intentions. As he stalked down the hallway in search of Lucy, he made himself the same promise that he'd made before. And before that.

Don't get too close.

But then there she was, huddled in her desk chair, her head in her hands. Now he discovered that it wasn't touching her that could make him break promises. Just looking at her could get him out of his safe, metaphorical corner.

"Lucy. Honey." He hurried forward and lifted her out of her chair to hold her against his chest. Her wavy hair tickled his chin as he tucked his head to press his cheek against hers. "It's going to be okay. No matter what happened, we'll find a way to fix it."

Her body was rigid against his. She wasn't crying, but there was the sound of sobs in her voice. "How are you going to fix *me?*"

She might as well have wrapped her fists around his heart and given it a brutal twist. He gathered her closer. "Lucy. Lucy…"

Over her head, a commotion from the open door to the reception area caught his attention. His tight chest eased. He moved his mouth to her ear.

"There once was a girl with a meeting/who thought that she'd taken a beating/but her boss knew the truth/it was the traffic, forsooth/and her self-doubting should have been fleeting."

Her head turned so their gazes met. "Traffic, forsooth?"

He couldn't help himself from grinning. "I'm out of practice, okay? But it's a limerick, and I never claimed to be good at them." Putting his hands on her shoulders, he turned her in the direction of the reception area. "Put your meeting face on, woman, because your volunteers await."

He could have left it at that. Certainly the way her face had brightened had alleviated his immediate worries. And he should have left it at that, he knew it, but Carlo was a detective after all, and unanswered questions tended to nag at him until he figured them out.

Lucy's behavior today was going to nag at him until he figured *her* out.

So, ninety minutes later, after they ushered the last of the volunteers from the offices, as well as a satisfied Claudia Cox, he handed Lucy her purse, turned off the office lights, then told her, firmly, that they were going out to dinner to celebrate.

He assumed she was dazed by the swing of emotions from failure to success because she was silent as he led her to his car and then to a nearby restaurant. She didn't seem to wake from her meeting afterglow until she'd had a couple of swallows of the martini he'd ordered for her.

Then she blinked, coughed a little and looked around her with the air of someone who'd been somewhere else until that moment. They were seated in an intimate booth, but Carlo had made sure to sit across from her and had angled his long legs so that they wouldn't brush Lucy's.

"Whoa. Wow." Now she peered at the drink and then took another sip. "Nice."

He bit back his smile. Knowing Lucy's habits after the weeks she'd been working for him, he had an idea that she'd gone lunchless again, which meant that martini was going straight from her stomach to her head.

"Have some bread sticks," he suggested.

She ignored him for a nibble at her alcohol-soaked olive. "It went well, don't you think?"

"Told you."

She waved that away with her plastic spear and then dumped it back in her drink before downing another swallow. "Don't be smug."

"That would be Claudia," he replied. "I can't say what's going on with her, but I think she has something up her sleeve. Every time she looks at you she gets this speculative gleam in her eye."

"Probably calculating how many calories I'll cost her when she gobbles me down," Lucy muttered.

He laughed. "Now you understand why I passed you off as my girlfriend that first night."

Her gaze sharpened as she lifted the martini once

again toward her mouth. "Okay, I get that. But what was that kiss about tonight? I thought—"

"I get to ask the questions," he interjected, because he'd be damned if he had an answer. "And my first one is why you immediately assumed when the volunteers didn't show that you'd done something wrong?"

She drained the rest of her martini and then their food arrived. Carlo was glad that she looked at her swordfish with some interest, then gave even more to her wineglass once the waiter filled it from the bottle Carlo had ordered.

Lucy was likely to get tipsy.

But that might get him the answers he wanted—and thus the distance from her he needed—that much quicker.

"Luce," he said as she set her wine down. "What happened back there?"

Her gaze slid away from him. "I don't know what you mean."

He topped off her glass and edged it closer to her hand. Okay, he was a bad man, but he'd rustle up some aspirin for her later. "You said Jason and Sam were right. That you're a failure."

A flush crawled up her neck, turning her face a pretty yet embarrassed pink. "Carlo…"

"I got to thinking about brunch after you said that. That morning when your thirtysomething-going-on-thirteen-years-old brothers were razzing you about copying pictures of your naked—"

"I've never done any such thing!" She had her glass in hand again and chugged more of her wine.

"I know. And when they mentioned it, I mostly dismissed it as some run-of-the-mill older-sibling teasing, but now I'm thinking there's more to the story."

She mumbled something into her glass.

"What?"

"I can't keep a job," she muttered, then drained her wine and looked up at him, her gaze defiant. "The first day I was at McMillan & Milano you said you heard I'd had some 'trouble' in Phoenix before coming back to San Diego. It wasn't man trouble like you guessed. It was trouble finding employment that…that I found satisfying."

She said that last as if it was a dirty, dark secret. "So, you didn't like a job," he responded. "So what? I'm not getting it."

Lucy cut her swordfish into bites, not one which made its way to her mouth. "I didn't like any of them. Over the past three years, I worked for a law firm, an elementary school district and at the corporate offices of a large health insurance company."

"Doing what?"

"I was an accountant, you know that. Numbers, columns, reports. Details. And I'm *good* with details."

There was a challenge in that last statement, too, as if she had to convince herself, as well as him. "I know you're good with details, Luce. I have no complaints on that score. None at all."

"Neither did any of my other employers." She was lifting her wineglass again. "But they didn't feel like the right fits. So I left each position hoping the next one would be better."

Her mouth turned down. "But maybe none of them

worked out because what I brought to those different jobs each and every time was *me*."

"Lucy." The dejection on her face would have cracked granite, and Carlo discovered with surprise that his heart wasn't nearly that hard. "Lucy, there's absolutely nothing wrong with you."

She was already shaking her head. "Suttons don't flounder. Suttons immediately find their launch pad and then rocket toward success."

"Jason and Sam—"

"Don't forget perfect Elise."

"You're not Elise—"

"Ya think?" Slumping against the back of her seat, Lucy closed her eyes. "Really, did you have to remind me?"

Oh, hell. Carlo couldn't even stand the thought of being a tabletop away from her. In a quick move, he scooted out from his side of the booth and tucked in next to her. She didn't seem to notice. "Lucy…" The back of his fingers stroked the silky skin of her cheek.

Her eyes opened, so wide. So blue. "What if nobody ever wants me?" she whispered.

"Sweetheart—"

There was a vulnerable little slur to her words as she spoke over him. The alcohol had apparently made its way upstream. "Don' tell, but I'm not sendin' out résumés." She spoke as if her tongue had thickened. "I'm 'voiding the want ads. The *A*'s in partcler. *A* is for Accounting, y'know that?"

"Yeah. I know that." He drew his fingers over her cheek again. "But maybe you're right to avoid accounting, Luce. Maybe what was wrong with those jobs wasn't you, but you with accounting."

She was shaking her head, but he was pretty sure she wasn't listening to him. "I'm accountant. I'm *an* accountant. That means I do number stuff. Details."

"Yeah…"

She jabbed herself in the chest with her thumb. "Good with details. I'm good with details."

"Yes. Yes, you are."

Her gaze narrowed. "You mean that?"

"I do, Lucy."

"Nice. Sooo nice." She sighed, then her head dropped to his shoulder. "You wan' me, don't you, Carlo? Tell me you wan' me."

His arm went around her shoulders and he dropped a kiss on the top of her fragrant hair. Oh, hell. "God help me, Lucy, I do. Yes, I do want you."

Chapter Ten

Outside the restaurant, as Carlo guided Lucy to his car, he decided against driving her to Elise and John's in her tipsy state. She'd had coffee, but still there remained a little wobble in her walk. Another cup of caffeine was needed, he told himself, and a place to drink it that was more comfortable and less public than the restaurant.

He suggested, she agreed, the car sped to his home.

Still, it surprised the hell out of him to find he was actually parked in his garage and that he was taking her by the hand and helping her out of the Lexus.

This wasn't a thinking man's move.

But the truth was, he wasn't ready to be apart from her just yet. He'd made up the coffee excuse when he was really acting on a whim instead of analyzing the life out of it instead.

When was the last time he'd done that?

When was the last time he'd felt so alive?

You want me, don't you, Carlo?

Those whispered words had acted like a defibrillator, restarting something inside him that had been deathly quiet for the past six years.

The living room felt chilled, so he bent to light the logs set in the fireplace. As they caught, he turned to Lucy, who stood in the center of the room, her arms at her sides, her big blue eyes trained on his face.

Now she didn't look drunk.

Not the tiniest bit tipsy.

You want me, don't you, Carlo?

She held her hand out to him, as if once again she'd seen inside him and heard his thoughts. She kept on doing that, didn't she?

That new living thing in his chest gave a strong jerk. That hand, those slim fingers, were an undeniable invitation. He wanted her; she wanted him. "Lucy... you're sure?"

"Aren't you, Mr. Milano?"

But this was no game, not this time, when the reflection of the flames was licking warmly at her skin just as he intended to. He opened his mouth to tell her, to make clear—what? His brain couldn't come up with a response.

He wasn't thinking again.

God, how he liked that.

His feet ate up the space between them. Then she was in his arms, the fabric of her dress cool against his palms, the body underneath it warm and pliable and so willing to press against him.

He felt a tremor run through her and he shuddered in response. "Lucy," he whispered, running his mouth from her temple to her jaw. "Lucy, Lucy, Lucy." Her head dipped like a flower on a stem so that he could explore the fragrant, smooth flesh of her neck.

He chased goose bumps to the vee over her breasts and felt her heart thudding against his mouth. His body was urging him on and he followed its impulses again, letting his hands roam over her back, her thighs, then up to cover her breasts. Beneath thin silk, her nipples tightened to points that he had to take into his mouth.

Her body arched as he did just that. He ran his tongue over fabric, wetting it, shaping her, then sucking hard, harder, because gentle wasn't alive enough for the man who now held Lucy. His thumb rubbed wet silk as he moved to the other breast and he reveled in the sweet sound of the breathy moans she made as he played with her.

Still, it wasn't enough.

His fingers found the zipper at her back and he drew it down, the sound an erotic hiss that was a counterpoint to their rough, matching breaths. The dress fell to the carpet with a plop, but he couldn't hear it, he couldn't hear anything but the whoosh-whoosh-whoosh of his blood as it galloped through him.

"Lucy," he breathed. Lucy, in a see-through bra, tiny panties, filmy stockings held up at the thighs by lace and a prayer. The high-heeled pumps on her feet only made the picture sexier.

More like a punch to the gut.

"You're so damn beautiful."

Another tremor ran through her body and he saw her sway. He took her in his arms and then bowed to impulse again and took her down to the carpet in front of the fireplace.

In the reflection of the fire, her skin glowed like the sunshine he'd called her. "You're still dressed," she whispered, her voice husky and low, a tantalizing stroke down his spine.

He shrugged out of his jacket and yanked off his tie, tossing them both away. Then, still in his shirtsleeves and slacks, he made a place for himself between her thighs. "Gotta keep something between us."

She frowned. "Carlo—"

He kissed the protest away. "Or it will be over too fast, baby."

When he lifted his head, her mouth was slack and her eyes were closed. He lowered again to tug on her bottom lip with his teeth, and his blood made another primal whoosh-whoosh-whoosh as she moaned and entwined her legs around his hips.

Clothes couldn't stop him from pressing his erection against the heated notch between her thighs. Nothing could stop him from kissing her again, penetrating her mouth with his tongue while his hips mimicked the action.

Lucy ground up against him, making him dizzy with lust.

He so wanted her.

He told her so, whispering it against her mouth. "You turn me on, so hard, so hot."

Her hips rolled from side to side and he groaned as

desire spread a mist over him. "I turn you on." There was a bubble of delight caught in her voice, reminding him of just how bright she made his world. "I like the sound of that."

"It's not a sound, baby," Carlo said, sliding lower on her body. "It's a touch." His cheek brushed against the tops of her breasts, and then he turned his head and stroked against her the other way. Her breath caught, he could tell as the mounds of her breasts rose and held there, swelling sweet and warm against his face. He wanted to bathe in her scent, wash himself in every sweet flavor she had to offer.

His hand was shaking—shaking!—as he worked the front catch of her bra and released her soft flesh. He lowered his head and caressed her new bareness with his cheeks. His chin rubbed against the furled buds of her nipples. Her hands held him there, her fingernails biting into his scalp until he caught her inside his mouth and sucked.

Her arms dropped to the carpet and her body lifted, a sacrifice to his pleasure. He lavished attention on her sensitive flesh, feeling the tension that tightened her muscles and yet left her at the same time boneless.

His tongue took a trip down the center of her, tucking inside her shallow navel and playing there, too, as she gasped for breath. He looked up past her wet nipples gleaming in the firelight to her kiss-swollen mouth and her half-open eyes.

She was desire embodied. Living, breathing lust that tasted like heaven. Carlo felt as if each of his pores was opening in order to take her in.

And now all he wanted to do was take her up, up, up, to give her back all the heat and air and precious feeling of being supremely alive that she gave to him.

"Pretty Lucy," he said, rolling to his side so he had better access to her half-naked body.

Cat-smiling, she turned toward him, but he pushed her flat again with his hand. "Stay where I can touch you."

She pouted, forcing him to lean down and nip at that pooched-out bottom lip. "Don't you want to feel good, baby?"

"I do feel good. I just don't feel enough of you."

But she let him slide her bra off her arms so that he could study the curves of her breasts and the sleek plane of her flat belly. Under his gaze, her stomach muscles trembled, and he placed his palm over them, insinuating his little finger beneath the elastic band of her panties that ran around her hips. Those muscles trembled again.

"Carlo." She sounded breathless as she tried rolling close again. "Let me."

He pushed her back down with his hand, a gentle touch, but one that allowed his pinkie to slide lower. It tangled in soft hair and he pictured them in his mind—golden curls that did little to hide the amazing folds and layers of her sex. He wanted to see that for real, and he would, but now it was so damn erotic to watch his big tanned hand disappear beneath the scrap of lace.

"Carlo." Lucy wiggled against the carpet. "I need you. Come inside me."

"I'm not done yet." He wasn't done with her. He had

to get done with her—the thinking part of him that he'd been smothering all night reminded him of that—and maybe this was the way to do it.

With her, parts of him that had been dead were alive again. But they were unfamiliar parts—maybe even unknown parts—and he wasn't sure it was smart to welcome their rebirth.

Maybe it would be best to bury them in pleasure, drown them in the ecstasy of Lucy's body, let them have this one wild ride, then shut them away before they led him into dangerous territory. He was still a cop at the core and the cop's instincts were sending out flares in warning.

Danger. Danger. Danger.

But now the heat of those flares only added to the burning light flickering against Lucy's skin and the conflagration roaring inside him. It was so damn hot, and he needed the liquid of her body to cool him down and quiet his clamoring heart.

As his fingers found the wet bud at the top of her sex, he stripped off her panties. He heard her swift intake of breath. "You're still dressed," she protested.

It didn't matter. He shifted between her legs and pushed them wide, then bent her knees to open her to him.

"Carlo!" She sounded anxious, maybe even panicky, but he slid his palms down her legs and gripped her ankles. It was *he* who was panicked. It was *he* who had to find a way to chill out and cool down.

He dropped his mouth to the opened petals of her sex. Her body jerked against his hold, but he only tightened his grip and breathed in her spicy, sweet taste. His tongue swiped the wet, private flesh.

She jerked again, made a strangled sound, wrapped her fingers in his hair. "Don't…stop."

Don't stop.

As if he could. As if one taste of her would somehow be the antidote to all this fiery desire. His mouth opened to taste more of her, to have more of her, to take into himself more, more, more.

His hands slid up her silky stockings to reach the even silkier texture of her inner thighs. He pushed against them, widening her to him, opening her so that he could get to everything. He had to have everything this time, satisfying that newly awakened Carlo so that after this he could return to his safe, dark hibernation.

Lucy was whimpering, pleading, moaning, mimicking the sounds that he was too preoccupied to make himself. They both sought release.

Lucy, from his sensual torture.

Him, from the terrible, beautiful light that was Lucy, and that was the thing that she'd awakened inside of him. Beneath his hands, her thigh muscles went rigid. Her hips lifted as she offered herself, gave him more, and he took it, took her firmly in his mouth and hoped that this shaking, quaking orgasm she offered up would be the single sacrifice the beast inside of him needed before going back to sleep.

Early the next morning, leaving Carlo to his apparent state of unconsciousness between his sheets, Lucy called John to pick her up. There were things she had to do that day, and getting to them without first waking the man she'd spent all night with seemed like the best plan.

Gathering her purse and her pumps, in bare feet she eased out onto the porch, prepared to wait for her brother-in-law, whom she'd sworn to secrecy.

But there was to be no waiting.

And no brother-in-law.

Lucy stared as her sister stormed up Carlo's front walk. "You could get a ticket driving that fast."

Elise halted on the step below Lucy, which left their eyes at the same level. Hers held a snap of blue fire. "The one in danger of unwanted trouble right now is not me."

Lucy sighed. "I know you think I'm—"

"I'm not talking about you," Elise said. "I'm talking about *him.*" Her gaze transferred to the closed front door, then she made a move to get past Lucy. "And I'm going to talk to him right this minute."

"Whoa." Lucy caught Elise's elbow. "Whoa, whoa, whoa. Where do you think you're going?"

"To tell that…that bounder to keep his mitts off my little sister."

Little sister has a thing for those mitts. Memory Lane beckoned, but Lucy stopped herself from taking that path. "What *is* a bounder, anyway? And why are you insinuating yourself into my business?"

Elise blinked. "I always insinuate myself into your business. It's the natural order of things. And I don't know what a bounder is, either. It just slipped out."

That's what I'm doing here, Lucy thought. *Slipping out.* "Let's go, Elise."

"And have you race off into the shower and then to work? No. If you're not going to let me at Carlo, then *we're* going to have a conversation. Right here. Right now."

The stubborn set of Elise's chin told Lucy all she needed to know. With a sigh, she dropped to the porch steps, tugging her sister down beside her. "You're an obstinate woman, that's what you are. Always have been. I remember when you knocked over Belinda Beall for passing those mean notes about me around elementary school."

Elise sniffed. "You asked for my help then, and admit it, that stringy-haired brat looked better than she ever had sitting on her butt in the dust."

"Yeah, but I didn't need, don't need—"

"Lucy…" Her sister turned her head to pin her with a laserlike set of blue eyes. "Don't give me that. Why did you move back home?"

"I… Well… Because…"

"You wanted family around to watch your back."

"Okay, maybe I did miss you guys, but I wasn't expecting to be treated as if I were ten."

"Goose—"

Lucy put her palm over her sister's mouth. "My point exactly. And while I'm accustomed to cringing over Jason and Sam using that nickname, I expected better of you."

Elise drew Lucy's hand away, then tucked her Grace Kelly hair behind her ears. "Come on. You'd be the first to kick someone in the ankles who was bothering me."

Sighing, Lucy slung her arm around her sister's shoulders. "That's a crack about my height, I know it is, but you're right. And you're right that I came home to be among family. But as an *equal* among them."

"Jase and Sam—"

"Will get their comeuppance one of these days, please God. It's another reason why I had to be here. To see those two overintelligent, overhandsome, crème de la overconfident big brothers of ours fall flat on their faces."

A little smile played around Elise's mouth. "You might be just in time."

"What?" Lucy goggled. "What are you talking about?"

"I just have one word for you. *Twins.*"

A shiver of delight tracked down Lucy's spine and she squirmed on the step. "No! You've set them up with twins? This is delicious."

"And entirely off topic. I came here to save you from Carlo."

Too late.

"But I see it's too late."

Lucy's gaze jumped to her sister. "Did I say that out loud?"

Elise shook her head. "You didn't need to. I can read it right on your face. You're in love with him."

"That's not true...." Her words trailed off. It was so, so true. Last night, in front of that fireplace, he'd slid into her body and slid straight into her heart. Right then, what had been a little seed—her years-old silly crush—had flowered into something more.

It wasn't just the lovemaking, which had been spectacular and sweet and serious and oh so unforgettable.

But that flower had been nurtured time and time again during the past weeks.

His giving her the Street Beat project.

The way he'd stuck up for her in front of her brothers, expressing publicly his confidence in her ability to do a job for him.

His support as she'd come apart at the seams when the volunteers were late.

When you thought about all that, no wonder she was in love with him.

"He doesn't want that from me, though," she whispered to Elise. "He likes his solitude. The way I feel won't fit."

Her sister made a wry face. "It's six-thirty in the morning. You've spent the night at the man's place. There must be some things he likes about you."

She tried to laugh, but it came out as more of a whimper. The night before, after he'd given her a spectacular climax while he was still fully dressed, he'd loosened his clothing, pulled on a condom, and then slid—hard and hot—inside her sated body. Despite the way her bones had been wax-soft, she'd found herself tilting into his thrust, wanting him as deep in her as she could bring him.

Braced on his elbows, he'd cradled her face with his hands. "This isn't going away, Luce, is it?" His thumbs had stroked over her cheekbones. "I want you more than the first time. I think I'll want you more when we're done this time."

She'd managed to shrug, because she'd hated that regret she could see lingering behind the desire.

"We're having some more fun. What's so wrong about that?"

His smile had been sad, his kiss soft. "Lucy, you know—"

"I know *you*," she'd said fiercely. "I know what you want and what you don't. I know myself."

"And you're just a girl who wants to have fun?" he'd questioned. "Really?"

She'd dragged down his head and lifted her hips high and let her body and her mouth finish the conversation.

"Luce?" Elise broke into the memory. "What are you going to do now?"

She stared at her bare toes. At her last pedicure, the manicurist had painted the teensiest little butterflies on her big toes. They floated in a sky of pale blue and looked ready to flutter off at any second. She could be like them. She could quit her position at McMillan & Milano. Fly away from Carlo. If she did so, even if she left her Street Beat project in the lurch, he wouldn't say a single word. He'd probably blame himself.

Of course he'd blame himself. Sober, responsible, noble Carlo Milano would think her defection was all his fault.

It was an easy out.

But hadn't she taken those much too often in the past twenty-five years? Hadn't she let Elise deal with Belinda Beall? Hadn't she let her brothers voice the obvious instead of taking a good look in the mirror? Hadn't the name Lucy Goosey been a too-true reflection of herself at—too many—times?

"Are you going to quit McMillan & Milano?" Elise was reading her mind again.

But the question prodded another memory to life. At the restaurant, under the influence of martinis and too much wine, she'd confessed to Carlo about her non-starter of a career. And not really paid much attention to what he'd replied.

But maybe you're right to avoid accounting, Luce. Maybe what was wrong with those jobs wasn't you, but you with accounting.

Was that where she'd gone wrong? Was her career a nonstarter because it wasn't the right career path after all?

She glanced over at Elise. "What do you think? I'm wondering if I should get out of accounting."

Her sister's eyes widened. A perplexed frown dug a line between her perfectly arched, golden eyebrows. "What are you talking about? You have a degree in accounting. You're an accountant."

And Elise was an actuary and Sam a banker and Jason an attorney.

Lucy could spell them all now, including accountant, but that didn't make her any better at her siblings' game. Her hand ran down the colorful paisley of her silk dress. It was dang hard to be the wild print in a family of tailored business suits. She'd tried for years to fit in, but then nothing had fit right.

"Lucy?"

The one interrupting her reverie this time wasn't her sister, but Carlo. Her head whipped around, and there he was, standing in his doorway.

Her stomach churned as she mentally cursed her big sister for her bossy ways. They were supposed to be long gone, because this was what she'd hoped to avoid: a confrontation with the man who'd stolen her heart before she'd figured out exactly how she was going to deal with the theft.

And now they had her sister as a witness.

Lucy snuck a glance at Elise, who had half turned toward Carlo, as well, and who even in the early morning looked unruffled and serene. Beautiful. Perfect. But he was ignoring Lucy's sister. His eyes were all for Lucy.

"Luce? What are you doing?"

Good question, huh? Her gaze took him in, from his rumpled short hair to his whiskered chin, to the jeans hanging low on his hips. His naked chest looked sexy and warm and solid.

Like something she could lean on.

Oh, man. How was she going to keep on working with him when she wanted so much more than he was willing to give?

"Carlo…"

At the sound of Elise's voice, Lucy started. In a quick movement, she grabbed her sister's wrist. Squeezed. "Let me," she murmured.

Elise sent her a searching glance. *I've got your back, little sister,* her look said.

But little sister was standing up. Lucy rose to her feet, just to prove it. And it was funny, she could stand up and face Carlo in this awkward moment *because of* Carlo. His confidence in her, the remembrance of his words, "I want you, Lucy," gave her the guts to…to…

What was she going to do? There was still that path of least resistance. That "I'm sorry I can't work with you any longer" excuse that would remove her from further pain.

He frowned at her. "Why were you sneaking away?"

Could she tell the truth? Could she say, "Because I'm in love with you"? But he didn't want to be a couple, and for his benefit she'd painted a picture of herself as a woman who didn't care about something so serious. It wouldn't be fair to him to alter that now.

So she pasted on her best, most upbeat smile and made the hard decision to stick with what she'd started. "Because today's a busy day and I wanted to get a jump on it. See you at the office."

Chapter Eleven

Germaine slipped her hand through Carlo's arm. "You've changed."

Startled, he stared down at her. "What are you talking about?"

"Something's different about you."

The thought unsettled him. With a frown, he gestured to their surroundings. "I can't imagine why you'd say so. I insisted we make a stop by the Street Beat site on our way back from our once-a-month lunch. You always complain I'm an obsessed workaholic and I've just proved your point."

Germaine's gaze shifted from his face to the immense stadium parking lot that was being turned into a two-million-square-foot festival venue suited to entertaining more than 75,000 ticket-holders over the following two days.

Everywhere you looked, equipment was stacked elephant-high and trucks were bringing in even more. Five stages were already under construction. Workers in hard hats crawled over and around them, while dueling boom boxes belted out each team's musical preference. A far section of the parking lot was cordoned off for the trailers that were now providing temporary headquarters for the concert promoter and Carlo's security people, and for others that would be used as lounge areas for the performers. The big names would have their own trailers towed in, and they'd left room for them in the area along with open spots nearby for the bands' tour buses.

One of his employees strode toward him, wearing a polo shirt with *McMillan & Milano* embroidered on the pocket and a harried expression. Others on his staff were at the venue, as well. "You're here!" Hank said. "Linda was looking for you earlier."

Carlo's eyebrows rose and he peered about, scanning the area for trouble. "Is there a problem?"

Hank shook his head. "No more than to be expected. But the fire marshal is on site and Logistics Linda thought you might want to speak with him."

All thoughts of Linda faded away as Carlo's attention caught on a small, slim figure in a pair of painted-on jeans, tennis shoes and another of the company's shirts, knotted at her waist. Lucy. He could see a slice of the small of her back between the end of the cotton and the beginning of midrise denim. Last night, he'd placed a hot, open-mouthed kiss right in that little dip. If he got close enough, would he see proof of his mark on her?

"Carlo?"

He yanked his attention back to Hank. "What?"

The other man sent an odd glance over his shoulder. "What's wrong?"

There once was a woman by my fire....

He cleared his throat. Forget the limerick. Forget the "mark." He hadn't marked Lucy. That sounded way too possessive for a man who kept his distance from other people. "Nothing's wrong. You came to me, remember?"

"Yeah. Linda. Fire marshal. Do you want to meet with him?"

Carlo shook his head. "That's on Linda. She's our go-to public services person. Or does she need me to address something we haven't foreseen?"

Hank's expression was puzzled. "No, as per usual, you've foreseen everything. It's just that...well, you generally want to, uh, have your hands on, uh, everything."

Carlo would *not* look Lucy's way again. "I don't know what you're talking about. I delegate."

"Recently, yes," Hank said. He backed up as if afraid he'd offended the boss. "And I only mean that in a positive way."

Carlo rolled his eyes and waved the other man off. "You'd think I was an ogre," he murmured to Germaine.

"Just a bit controlling," she said sweetly. "But it looks like I'm right. Even your employees have noticed the change."

Carlo didn't want to think about it. He put on his

most charming smile. "Maybe I didn't want to interrupt this opportunity to spend time with the most enchanting woman in San Diego."

Germaine's laugh was good to hear. "I haven't seen that magnetic grin of yours in years. I am now curious as can be to know where you found it after all this time."

In Lucy's eyes. On a roller coaster. In front of a crackling fire. *As I slid into Lucy's sweet body and felt her welcome all the way to my soul.*

Without thinking, his gaze traveled to where he'd last seen her. There she was, chatting like a magpie, her hands moving with the same energy and grace she brought to everything. Her job. Lovemaking.

"I like that smile even better."

Carlo started. He'd forgotten all about Germaine until she'd spoken, but she was right, he could feel the smile curving his mouth.

Germaine touched his arm again. "She sent me a get-well present, you know. Lucy, I mean."

It didn't surprise him. "Chocolate? Flowers?"

"A kitten."

"What?" Germaine had been waiting on her porch when he'd picked her up so he hadn't spotted any new resident at 247 Cavendish Drive. "That's kind of…"

"Exactly what I needed," she finished for him. "And she said that if it didn't appeal she had another good home for the dear thing. But the idea *did* appeal. You see, the night you two dropped by she noticed this framed photo I have of the cat Pat and I had when we were first married. I'd happened to mention how Serpico kept me company at home on the long night shifts, and I suppose..."

"She remembered." Carlo rubbed his palm over his breastbone.

"I think she saw that I need company now, too."

Lucy *would* see that. Lucy saw so much. Her instincts about people were well honed and as far as he was concerned, wasted on ledgers and spreadsheets. Sure, she was good with details, but that didn't mean she had to lock all her light away in shadowy cubicles for the rest of her life, crunching numbers.

That kind of thing suited him far better than it did Lucy.

He preferred being locked away in the shadows.

"I'd like to tell her how the newest member of my family, Kojak, is getting on," Germaine said, starting across the blacktop.

"No," Carlo instantly responded.

Germaine blinked. "No?"

"I mean, she's probably busy." Suddenly he didn't want to get too close to Lucy. The lovemaking had been brain-blowing and he'd been glad when Lucy had dragged her sister away this morning. He'd yet to get his mind around what was happening between them—not to mention how he was going to explain all this to Lucy's sister, and probably, at some point, her brothers, too. He couldn't explain it to himself! He couldn't explain why each time they were together, each time she tried to pass it off as "fun," he was left unsatisfied at some level, even though his body was humming with satisfaction.

A thread of panic iced his blood. What was happening to him? "I'll give you Lucy's cell phone number, Germaine. You can call her later."

"Oh, you're probably right," Germaine replied. "It looks to me as if she's very busy with that young man with the long hair and tattoos."

Carlo's blood ran colder. He swung around, squinting to get a sharper view. Oh, yeah. There was Lucy, animated, smiling, her small hand on the arm of that... that...tool.

"Wrench," he spit out.

Germaine slanted him an inquiring glance.

"Have you ever heard of Silver Bucket?"

"Nooo."

"Me, neither." It was gratifying not to be the only nonfan, though he supposed that did put him squarely in the fuddy-duddy category. "Let's go."

"Go where?"

He was already heading across the blacktop. "I thought you wanted to talk to Luce."

Okay, it looked as if Germaine was swallowing her smile. Damn. "Didn't you?" he pressed.

"Right." Germaine lengthened her stride to keep up with him. "This is all my idea."

Carlo slowed. "Sorry, I walk fast."

"I don't mind. Pat did, too."

Pat. At the mention of the man's name, Carlo's step hitched. What would his old partner think about the company they'd envisioned together? The one that Carlo used to fill his days and nights?

Gotta find some balance, boy. It was as if his mentor was speaking directly into his ear. *All work and no play...*

And he'd been playing with Lucy, hadn't he? Having his fun? But again, that term just didn't sit well with him. Nor did the way that Wrench was slinging his skinny, tattooed arm around Lucy to drag her nearer his concave chest.

It reminded him of what he'd learned at that Street Beat party weeks ago. The band was famous for its pyrotechnics show. Since that had been forbidden during the San Diego festival, perhaps Wrench was looking for a substitute with some fireworks with Lucy. The thought made him want to break something.

Wrench's drumstick-thin forearms would work.

He halted in front of the two, but they were so absorbed in each other it didn't appear they realized he and Germaine had arrived.

It pissed him off. "I'm not paying you to make out with the talent."

She froze, and Wrench's scrawny arm slid away. With a frown between her brows, she turned to him.

A delighted smile broke over her face as her attention shifted to his left. "Germaine! How's Kojak?"

"Wonderful. Thank you so much again."

Lucy leaned in for a quick hug, then introduced the older woman to the lead singer. Next, she gestured toward Carlo with a careless hand. "I don't believe you've met this charmer. My boss, Carlo Milano."

He was forced to shake hands. "Wrench," the man said.

No last name. Figured.

"You should probably let Lucy get back to her work," Carlo said, trying to sound pleasant.

Apparently he didn't pull it off too well because Lucy glared at him. "What? Now you don't trust me to do my job?"

He wanted to groan. Damn it, what was wrong with him? He *was* different. The old Carlo, while not particularly friendly, wasn't bad tempered. The old Carlo could be perfectly civil, even to a rock star named Wrench, no matter what woman he was touching— even his own.

No! Lucy was not his woman.

He tried to make amends. "Sorry, sorry," he said to them both. "This close to the big festival, I get a little edgy."

Wrench nodded. "Lucy, too. I was just persuading her that tonight, after we wrap up the first evening, that she needs to relax. I'm having a big party at my hotel suite. There's a private whirlpool tub and we'll have music, eats, the whole works. You two are welcome to come."

His gaze included Germaine, which meant that he assumed Lucy was already on board with the plan.

Oh, yeah, Carlo thought. He was different now. Really, really different. Because the idea of Lucy in a private whirlpool tub with the tool-of-the-moment was not something he could accept, even if it meant he was leaving his safe, comfortably dark corner.

"Sorry," he told the singer, grinding his back teeth through a fake smile. "But Lucy and I already have plans for after the festival tonight."

At 2:00 a.m., Lucy was still moving around the spacious McMillan & Milano security trailer, afraid that if she stopped, her legs would freeze up altogether. Gathering half-empty water bottles and disposing of stale baskets of pretzels and crackers gave her mental processes time to unwind after the hours of intense focus.

One night at the Street Beat festival required more of her brain than a week in an accountant's office at tax season. But her mind was downshifting now that the night was concluded, leaving her in a pleasant, zoned-out state of tired satisfaction.

She heard the trailer's door open and close but didn't look up, hoping whoever it was wasn't looking for any intelligible conversation from her. After the last few hours, she couldn't give one more opinion or make one more decision. Unless the new person in the trailer wanted to silently gnaw on some leftover crackers, they were out of luck.

Better yet, maybe they'd be content with taking a dented half-full bottle of water and going away.

"Lucy."

At the sound of that voice, her hand tightened, crackling the plastic in her hand. Carlo. Oh, she was much too tired to figure out how to play him tonight.

Did he want the sympathetic friend? The light-hearted lover? The easy-to-please employee who wouldn't ask for any more than he was willing to give from the distance of his dark corner?

"You don't have to do that cleanup. Let it wait until tomorrow."

Without looking at him, she continued her tidying. "My volunteers are responsible for at least some of this mess."

"Your volunteers did a great job tonight."

Her head lifted and she found the energy to smile. "They did, didn't they?"

He nodded. Though he'd spent more time on the site than she had, the only signs of his long hours were the evidence of dark whiskers on his face and his loosened tie. But his shirt was still a pristine white, and his navy blazer looked as if it had just emerged from a dry cleaner's plastic.

Lucy, on the other hand, felt as wilted as the daisies someone had placed in a glass bowl on the trailer's kitchenette counter. She tossed the bottle in her hand into the trash bag at her feet and then ran her hands along her jeans, as if she could give them a little starch with the touch of her palms.

"You know, you've caused me a big problem," he went on. His expression was serious. Too serious.

Lucy's heart bobbed up and down like a yo-yo. No. She was too tired for this. Their relationship, or nonrelationship, or whatever it was or wasn't, couldn't be a topic of conversation tonight. That little fog of fatigue wasn't lifting in her brain, not at all, and she'd need each one of her faculties to find the right role to act for him.

She licked her lips, wondering how she could put him off. "Carlo…"

"I'm going to have to redo the financials on the Street Beat festival to account for the gigantic bonus check I'm going to write you tomorrow night."

She stared at him.

He smiled, and if she didn't know he didn't have any

soft spots inside of him, she'd say the smile looked tender. "Luce, you've got to realize that your volunteers did a bang-up job because *you* did a bang-up job."

Her throat felt tight. "You think so? You really think so?"

"Yeah. I really think so. As do Hank, and Linda, and Fernando and all the other McMillan & Milano staff who worked here tonight. Not to mention Claudia. Apparently a contingent of the parents corralled her and thanked her for your professionalism and dedication."

Lucy's tired legs finally gave up the ghost and she found herself dropping to the trailer's couch. "Well, that was nice of them."

Carlo shook his head. "People don't go out of their way just to be nice. They go out of their way when their experience exceeds their expectations." He paused, then strode over to sit on the coffee table facing her. Their knees nearly touched. "You sure as hell exceeded mine."

Lucy backed farther into the corner of the couch. Oh, what did that mean? That wasn't a segue to a place she didn't want to go, was it? "Um, uh…"

"I didn't think the volunteers would do anything more than get in the way, at best. Instead, you assessed, organized and charmed that clutch of adults and teens into a working crew that made a difference tonight— both for McMillan & Milano and for the concert-goers."

It was maybe the second-longest speech Lucy had heard Carlo make in the past weeks and it was about her job performance. Her excellent job performance.

Lucy sat a little straighter, letting his evaluation join

with her own sense of a job well done. Satisfaction heightened into bliss. "I appreciate the compliment. And the confidence you had in me in the first place when you assigned me the project. That meant a lot."

"You can do anything you put your mind to, Luce. You can have anything you really want. I know that. I hope tonight's shown you that."

"Yes." Lucy found herself nodding. Lucy Goosey had finally, for once and for all, flown the coop and left Lucy the capable in her place. "Thanks again for the opportunity to learn that." Her head dropped back to the cushion and she closed her eyes. "But there's still another day of the festival to go."

"Our last day to work together."

That's right, Lucy thought, drifting on the waves of fatigue rolling through her head. Come Monday, Carlo's secretary would be back on the job and Lucy would be back sifting through the want ads. She'd appeased her guilt in the past week by telling herself she was too busy with Street Beat to seek out another position, though on Monday she'd have to start seriously looking.

But I'm not limiting myself to accounting positions, she thought, suddenly certain. *I'm good with details, but I'm good with people, too, and maybe I can find a way to use both those talents.*

"So I told Wrench we had plans tonight," Carlo said, interrupting her reverie. "What would you like to do?"

She cracked one eye open. "Do I look like a woman ready to do anything? I know why you said that to Wrench. Don't worry about actually following through with it."

He frowned. "What do you mean? Why do you think I told Wrench we were doing something?"

She had to open both eyes to roll them, and she managed, despite the fatigue weighing down her lids. "I grew up with Jason and Sam, two of the most over-protective males on the planet. They would have heard the words *party* and *whirlpool tub,* and considering the rock singer source, gone on to tell him anything, up to and including an audience with the president of the United States, to prevent me from hanging out in Wrench's hotel suite. Though for the record, I can handle Wrench just fine. And by the way, he invited my volunteers on stage for his last set tomorrow night. That's pretty great of him, don't you think?"

Carlo's expression blanked. "You…" He took a breath and started again. "You…"

"First things first," she heard him mutter. "Are you saying you think of me like your brothers?"

The tired fog in Lucy's head was making it hard to interpret his tone. "Um, close enough."

He muttered something else. Something possibly obscene. "Hell, Lucy." He rose to his feet, forking a hand through his short hair. His gaze sharpened on her face. "I'm not one of your damn brothers."

"O-kay."

Apparently that wasn't the response he was hoping for because he turned to pace around the room. "I don't feel the least bit brotherly toward you."

"O-kay."

He took another turn around the small space. "Fine. Whatever." It sounded as if he was having an argument with himself. He lifted a hand, let it drop to his side, then he halted in the middle of the room and trained his gaze on her again. "You handling Wrench is not something I find myself keen to think about. At all."

"O-kay." Again.

"As a matter of fact, we're going to have to come to an understanding here, Lucy. About us."

Oh, no.

Now, *that* sounded like what she wanted to avoid. Her brain was spent, her body was all out of energy, there was nothing left inside her right now to deal with this particular person in the particularly right way. "Tomorrow—"

"Now," he bit out. "Right now."

"Carlo—"

"It isn't fun anymore, Lucy. Last night, for your information, was *not fun*."

She drew back, wishing the couch cushions could absorb her and that she'd simply disappear. Her mind spun, but as it was weighed down by her tiredness, it only gave a couple of drunken revolutions as it tried to find a way that this wasn't a rejection of her.

"We can't keep meeting 'accidentally' in my bed. Not for *fun*. Would you agree with that?"

Lucy couldn't keep up with the words tumbling from his mouth. "I don't know what you mean. What you want…"

"What I want…" He mumbled that under his breath, too. "What I want doesn't seem to matter so much anymore."

Lucy sucked in a breath, trying to focus on what Carlo was saying and how he was acting. Did he want her to be the nonthreatening, nonsexual Goose again? Was that it? Was Ms. Sutton no longer welcome in his life? Between his sheets?

The thought shouldn't feel like a stab to her heart. She'd always known what they had was as temporary as her position at McMillan & Milano. If she now wanted more, it was her own dumb fault. Everybody knew you didn't get over a crush by going to bed with one.

And once you realized it was more than a crush and was really love…

Stupid, Lucy, she thought, staring at the clenched fingers in her lap. Stupid, stupid, stupid.

"Here's the deal, Lucy."

She looked up to see Carlo cross his arms over his chest. "We're going to have to formalize our casual relationship."

"Huh?"

"Everyone's noticing it. Commenting upon it. I've been in a better mood. Easier to work with. Less intense. That's you. That's your influence. I like it."

She couldn't think of what to say.

"And I like you in my bed. I don't want it to be an occasional 'lapse.' You shouldn't want that for yourself, either. So we'll…I don't know…start seeing each other on a more regular basis."

"Starting Monday, I'm not going to be working for you anymore," she pointed out, still trying to keep up with him.

He shrugged. "We'll make time around our schedules. Next week I'm booked pretty solid, but maybe we could meet for a drink on Thursday. Around ten?"

Really, she was so exhausted from the evening and the odd roller coaster ride of the last few minutes that she could hardly form words. "At 10:00 p.m.?"

"You could spend the night with me," he said.

"I could spend the night with you."

A little smile quirked the corners of his mouth. "So I lied. It *was* fun the other night and I want it to be that way again. You told me you're a girl who wants to have fun and I'm more than willing to provide that."

So this is what she'd wrought. With all her twisting and turning to make what happened between them comfortable for Carlo, for all the times she'd worked so hard not to scare him away, she'd contorted herself into the position she found herself in right now.

And all she could think of was that she didn't know how to play the moment.

How to play the moment.

How to *play the moment*.

How to be something she was not.

Like all the years she'd played accountant, taking on a role with Carlo was just as, ultimately, unsatisfying. Heartbreaking.

He'd given her the confidence to look beyond her training to a new kind of career. Now she'd have to find the courage to tell Carlo Milano what Lucy Sutton really wanted for her life.

"I don't want to formalize our casual relationship," she said, her heart beating loud in her ears. "I'm sorry, but I don't want a casual relationship with you at all."

"What?" His eyes narrowed. "You don't want me?"

Funny, he didn't look like he believed that. "No. I don't want you casually at all."

He took a step back. "You know, you know…I don't—"

"Do the couple thing. I do know that."

"Damn it, Lucy, you said…you acted as if…"

"I could be as casual about things as you. As careless—"

"I was *never* careless with you."

"You're right, you're right."

"What happened to the girl who said it wasn't serious?"

For some reason, Lucy thought of the perfect Elise. Despite his denial, was that who he wanted? Would he have wanted to be a couple if Lucy was more like Elise? But she'd been whatever everyone else wanted for too long. The silly younger sister, the sexy temporary secretary. Now it was time to be what Lucy wanted for herself.

"That girl…that girl is really someone who should have been more honest with you and with herself. I want more. I want it all. And, thanks to you and what I've learned through working at McMillan & Milano, I now know I'm good enough, talented enough and, well, *woman* enough to reach for all my dreams."

"Lucy." Carlo ran a hand down his face. "Damn it, Lucy." Now, finally, he sounded as tired as she felt. And as if he truly understood the situation. Understood what she was saying. "I didn't mean to…I didn't see—"

"You didn't do anything wrong, not really." He was still the star of so many of her sweet dreams. He was still the man who had given her this newfound confidence. She dredged up a smile for him. It wasn't his fault that he couldn't give her any more than that.

"I'm in love with you. But I don't want a casual relationship. I want a man of my own, and someday I hope I'll find him."

Chapter Twelve

Carlo stalked through the late-night crowds attending the Street Beat festival, the relentless drum rhythm from the nearest stage too close to the throb of a toothache. Less than an hour remained before the festival closed, and it couldn't come quick enough for him. He always grew antsy as an event came to an end, whether it was a charity golf tournament or a holiday parade, but tonight his cop instincts were as palpably on alert as the raised hairs on the back of his neck.

A big hand clapped between his shoulder blades. "There you are."

Startled, Carlo swung around to face the two blond men grinning at him. "What the hell—" Recognizing Lucy's brothers, Jason and Sam, he tried to relax. "I didn't know you guys were coming!"

"With dates." Jason fumbled through the introductions, and it was obvious he wasn't entirely clear on which of the identical women with them was which. "Allie and Jane...or Jane and Allie...this is Carlo Milano."

The twins didn't seem surprised that Jason couldn't keep then straight. "Allie," one said, squeezing his hand with a strong grip. The other gave a shy wave. "Jane."

They were both medium height, with willowy figures and medium-brown hair threaded with auburn. Each wore their hair in a chin-length style that wisped around their heart-shaped faces. Even as a trained observer, and Carlo considered himself a damn good one, if dressed identically these two would even be hard for him to individualize.

"Elise set us up," Sam confided. "This is the first time we've been out together."

"It's nice to meet you both," Carlo said, nearly having to shout as the music grew louder. "Hope you're having a good time."

Sam's mouth moved, but he couldn't hear his reply. "What?"

Leaning closer, Sam spoke directly into his ear. "We're on the lookout for Lucy. Have you seen her?"

Carlo nodded. In his dreams all last night. At least every fifteen minutes all today and this evening. As much as he'd wanted to keep his distance from her, she kept flitting into his consciousness or into his line of sight.

What was it about butterflies that always lifted a man's mood?

"I called her early this morning to tell her we'd be

here tonight, but she practically bit my head off," Sam continued, frowning. "Something about not needing a keeper. You know anything about that?"

"I don't know anything about her," Carlo muttered. She'd completely flummoxed him last night in the trailer. After three weeks under the spell of her bright personality, accented by two nights of her silky body in his arms, he'd thought he understood Lucy. He'd thought he understood what Lucy wanted from him. And that she understood exactly how much—how little—he was looking for himself.

And he'd made it clear every step of the way, hadn't he? Up to and including last night in the trailer. *I want to formalize our casual relationship.* Okay, even to himself that made him sound like an ass, but the sentiment was honest.

He'd been honest with her.

An anger he'd been trying to suppress rose from his belly and fired a burn in his chest. There was a name for women who turned the tables on a guy like that. And it wasn't Butterfly.

Man-eater. That was it. He'd thought she was sweet, but boy, was he wrong! His anger ratcheted higher. A woman like Lucy said what she had to, did what she had to, to turn the male of the species upside down and inside out, making him so confused that he was easy prey.

Once he was down, she'd go for all the tasty internal organs. She'd go for the heart.

Too bad for her that Carlo didn't have one.

And lucky for him.

The two couples in front of him were exchanging

puzzled glances. "What?" he questioned, raising his voice. *"What?"*

Jason gave him an awkward pat on the shoulder. "You okay, friend? You seem a little, uh, moody."

"If by 'moody' you mean black looks and dark mutters," Sam added. "So we'll leave you to it, if you'll just point our way to Goose."

Goose. That was the damn problem. She'd waltzed into his office three weeks before and he'd remembered her as the sweet, soft, silly little Goose. His memories had left him unprepared for the sharp, sexy, grown-up female who had yanked him out of his dark corner only to tumble him onto his butt.

Yeah, baby, he thought, anger spiking again. *Thanks for that one hell of a trip and fall.*

Jason was staring at him again. "Goose," he prodded. "Remember her?"

"Forget that man-eater?" Carlo ground out. "Never."

Her brothers glanced at each other. Sam mouthed, *Man-eater?* Then their gazes swung Carlo's way again and brightened to matching lasers. "What's going on?" one said. "What have you done to Goose?"

"She's not a goose," Carlo snapped back. "For God's sake, at least get that straight. Your sister is a grown, capable woman, a…a…" *Man-eater.* But hell, he liked his nose just as it was so he wouldn't risk repeating that again.

"She can take care of herself." He faced Sam. "And she doesn't need you undermining that at every opportunity with talk of her photocopying her butt."

Jason lifted a finger. "Oh, I think that was me."

Carlo shook his head. "Never mind. You're idiots,

I'm an idiot, and as a matter of fact, if we've got an XY chromosome set, I'm beginning to think we're all doomed to idiocy."

The more assertive twin, Allie, grinned. "I think I like your friend," she said to the brothers.

Carlo huffed out a sigh, then the band on the closest stage swung into another song with a headache-inducing beat that drummed pain into his brain. Would this night never end? "Let me show you where Lucy is," he shouted over the noise. "She's over by Stage 5. Silver Bucket is performing there."

"Oh," Allie said, nudging her sister with her elbow. "Let's go. We're going to see that hottie, Wrench."

Wrench. Carlo ground his teeth as he led the small group toward the far stage. He supposed Lucy would find her way to the singer's party suite that night. If only to thank him for letting her volunteers up on stage with him for his last set.

Who was he kidding? A man-eater would go after Wrench because she was always hungry for more.

That fire in his chest burned hotter. It was like an ulcer, chewing at his insides with feral teeth. Pushing his way through the concert-goers, he was finally halted by the wall of people gathered around the stage to hear Silver Bucket play. He was fifty yards away, and he was grateful for his height, which allowed him to see over the fans who were all on their feet and swaying or dancing to the music's beat.

Near the front of the stage, people were packed like sardines and Carlo's cop sense started quivering again, harder. His people were down there, trained security personnel who were built like bar bouncers, and they should be able to keep the excited crowd in order. Still, something didn't feel right, especially when he couldn't see Lucy and her volunteers anywhere. He didn't want them stuck in the middle of an amped-up mob. His fingers found the walkie-talkie clipped to his waist and brought it to his mouth so he could call an extra contingent of security to Stage 5.

As he clicked off, he saw Lucy and a small group of teenagers appear onstage, behind and to the left of the drummer. Relief trickled through his tension.

Okay. There. She wasn't packed in with the gyrating multitude where an errant elbow or knee could bring her slight self down to the blacktop. On the stage, there was nothing more dangerous than a heavy metal rock band and their instruments.

The current song they were playing died out, but they segued immediately into the next. The crowd screamed in an ululating cry of approval. The twin named Allie was close enough that he could hear her yell to Sam and Jason, explaining why the fans were going nuts. "This is their big hit," he heard her yell. "'Mosh Pit.'"

Carlo's stomach knotted as he saw the fans swarm forward, eliminating all the space between their bodies. Wrench yelled something unintelligible into the microphone and the crowd let out another screaming reply.

Carlo didn't wait to see what would happen next. Intending to make it to the stage come hell or high water, he started off.

A hard hand caught his elbow. Jason. "Where's Lucy?"

Carlo could read the other man's lips but couldn't hear a sound over the noise around him.

He pointed on the stage, then his heart froze. She wasn't there.

Where had she gone? His gaze darted around the musicians and their instruments as he tried to locate her.

The fire inside him leaped higher, roasting the place where his heart would be if he'd allow himself to have one. Damn it! Damn it! If she hadn't bewitched him with her infectious laughter, with the way she saw inside him, he wouldn't be feeling this knife edge of panic.

If she wasn't such a temptress—a man-eater—

Oh. Oh, thank God. There she was.

His heart—that heart he wasn't supposed to have— slammed like a knocking fist against his chest wall. *Hello? Hello? Is anyone alive in there?*

And he was alive. More alive than he'd been since Pat's death, he realized. He felt each beat thump inside his chest and felt the muscle work to push his blood through his system. His hot blood. His undetached, undistanced blood rushing through a body that could no longer fool itself about what had happened to him in the past three weeks.

Man-eater. Hah. How could he have even thought such a stupid thing about her for even an instant?

He knew what was eating at him now.

Despite how comfortable he'd been in the shadows, how easy he'd found it before to keep clear of those living and breathing around him, he'd gone ahead and fallen in love with sweet sunshine. With Lucy.

Sam's hand tightened on his arm. Carlo swung his head toward him.

Her brother's mouth moved again. *Lucy?*

Carlo turned back toward the stage, where he'd seen her half-hidden by a tower of speakers. But before he could point her out, explosions erupted from both sides of the stage. Jets of light streamed skyward, while white clouds billowed, obscuring the musicians—and Lucy and her volunteers.

The pyrotechnics. The band known for their light and fire and smoke display had not held to their contractual promise—and instead had unleashed potential disaster.

Carlo didn't remember moving. One minute he was blinking to dispel the after-dazzle in his eyes, and the next he was halfway through the packed crowd. Halfway, but not close enough to Lucy.

The sound of the crowd was so loud they were drowning out the music of the band and there was barely breathing space between each body. Carlo saw his beefy security guys still holding strong at the front of the stage, but the first fifty feet of people standing that near had turned the "Mosh Pit" song into a reality.

As he pushed closer, gaining inches only to be shoved back a foot by the raucous crowd, he saw that Wrench was encouraging the craziness by the way he stood on the stage's edge and sang to the first few rows, his bare-chested body bent at the waist.

A girl popped out of the melee like a jack-in-the-box, trying for a kiss from Wrench. When she didn't make her target, the group threw her up again.

"Damn it," Carlo muttered, pushing through the people around him with new strength. His front-of-stage security couldn't last long without reinforcements, or without Wrench and the rest of Silver Bucket doing something to calm the crowd.

But nothing could calm him, not when he saw Lucy rush toward the lead singer and grab the microphone out of his hand. Positioned at the very edge of the stage, she was saying something to him, then shouting into the microphone, pleading with the crowd, he realized, to quiet down. The whole place was a riot of sound and movement.

Then another explosion sent sparklers of white fire across the stage. The crowd screamed and moved farther forward, arms outstretched, reaching for the band. Panic closed Carlo's throat as he realized his security team couldn't hold out against the wave of rabid fans, their excitement driven high by the forbidden pyrotechnics.

And Lucy was still up there, so close to the edge, now handing the microphone to Wrench, who seemed to have come to his senses. He put his arm around Lucy's waist, as if about to drag her away from the dangerous brink of the stage...

But it was too late.

Time stilled for Carlo, the way it did whenever adrenaline flooded his system. The cacophony around him receded, and it was quiet as death except for the heavy pound of his pulse.

He remembered finding Pat lying on the sidewalk. He remembered the slick and hot feel of the older man's blood between his fingers as he tried to staunch the flow and save his life. He'd lost that battle.

And he'd lose Lucy like he lost Patrick. He could see it all slipping away from him. Her butterfly brightness, her sparkling laughter, their love that could have lit his way for the rest of their lives. He felt it slipping away just as he saw a hand reach up from the pulsing crowd to wrap around her ankle. Just like that, Lucy slipped over the side of the stage and down, down, down, until she was swallowed by the wild throng.

This was why you didn't love people, he thought, pushing forward even as his heart was trampled.

This was why he refused to love. It could hurt so damn bad. It could make you so damn weak.

Someone was inside Lucy's head trying to get her attention by banging both fists on her skull. She squeezed her eyes tighter shut and tried to go back to sleep, but now the someone had a voice besides those insistent knuckles.

The voice sounded like her mother's.

Lucy allowed her eyelids to lift halfway. That was her mother, all right, with a worried frown between her brows. The back of her fingers felt cool against Lucy's cheek. "Honey? How are you feeling?"

"There's a dwarf inside my brain who wants out," she mumbled.

"That's our Goose." It was Sam, sounding a little worried himself. "Other girls fantasize about movie stars, but she dreams of dwarfs."

She turned her head on the pillow to find him with her gaze, and winced at the movement. "Take it easy, honey," her mom said. "Slow and easy."

This time, Lucy moved just her gaze instead of her whole head. Mom, Dad, Sam and Jason. There was a big bouquet of flowers on one of those skinny little hospital tables….

She was in a hospital bed. In a hospital room. Her hand lifted to brush the hair away from her face, but she discovered her arm was too heavy to move.

She frowned at it.

Jason piped up. "We thought you'd like pink."

She was wearing a pink cast on her forearm. Lucy lifted her gaze to her mother's face.

Laura Sutton didn't need more prodding. "Honey," she said. "You broke your wrist and you received a slight concussion when you fell—well, were pulled—from the stage."

Street Beat. Silver Bucket. The pyrotechnics, "Mosh Pit." The real mosh pit in the crowd.

Lucy closed her eyes. She'd brought her volunteers into the midst of all that. Her stomach contracted as she remembered the acrid smell of the white smoke and the frightened faces of the teenagers who moments before she'd happily ushered onto the stage. Not long after, she'd thought the crowd was about to break through security and leap up to overrun the musicians and everyone else.

"Was…" Her throat was so dry, she had to swallow and start again. "Was anyone else hurt?"

"No." It was her dad who spoke up now, and she knew to trust him. Mom might have tried to soft-pedal the truth, but her father would always give it to her straight. "There were a few squished toes and torn shirts in the crowd from what we understand, but the only one who required a hospital visit was you."

Her chest loosened a little. "And my volunteers? I had a list in the trailer. Are we sure they're all accounted for?"

"Carlo mentioned something about it," her dad affirmed. "He said they were all fine."

Carlo. The dwarf in her head started on her skull again, using hammers *and* fists this time. What flack was McMillan & Milano going to have to take for the debacle? She'd been right there, and with her *volunteers*. Shouldn't she have seen evidence of the fireworks that were about to go off? Shouldn't she have been able to keep her volunteers far from any potential danger?

Carlo was never going to talk to her again, even though he'd likely already sworn never to talk to her again, anyway. The new churning in her stomach made a nauseating counterpoint to the banging in her head.

Someone tapped on the door. A nurse. "You're awake, Lucy. There's a Claudia Cox out here insisting on seeing you. Do you feel up to it?"

Lucy felt up to finding a hole in the ground, lying down in it and pulling the dirt in after her. But Claudia didn't take no for an answer, which was actually something Lucy really admired about her. "I'll see her," she said.

Jason moved to sit on the end of her bed. The legs of Sam's chair squeaked against the linoleum as he edged closer to her. "Good God, Goose. You're going to talk to her now? She'll rip you to shreds."

"I'd like to see the woman try it," Jason replied, his expression grim. "Lucy might have made herself another mess, but nobody but us has a right to say that. Goose has got backup."

Lucy sighed. Goose had backup, all right, and as she looked at their concerned faces and protectively squared shoulders, she found it hard to resent Jason's comment that "Lucy might have made herself another mess." Because she had.

Chanel No. 5 reached her before Claudia did. Then she was there, ignoring every other person in the room to focus on Lucy. "There she is," she declared, sliding a gold box of Godiva chocolates next to the flowers on that skinny table. "The woman who I—"

"Now, just a minute," said Jason, in his best tight-ass attorney's voice.

Claudia kept on talking. "—am hoping will take a job in my offices starting next week."

"It's not her fault," Jason said, as if Claudia's startling offer had not been voiced. "I know it might look like that, but—"

Claudia's scathing glance would have melted a lesser man. "It didn't look like her fault at all. Were you even there?"

"Well, um, I was, but we couldn't see anything because of the smoke, and the, um, uh…"

"That's because Silver Bucket broke their contract by bringing in those pyrotechnics. They not only caused all that smoke and confusion, but they also set off the crowd and caused a dangerous situation. A dangerous situation that your sister was instrumental in defusing."

Jason blinked. "Well, um, uh, we couldn't see anything, as I said. There was that smoke, and the, um, uh…"

Lucy took pity on him. "Shut up, Jason. You were saying, Claudia? You might have a position for me in concert promotion?"

"For someone who handles details and people the way you do? For someone who knows music and is quick on her feet? For someone whom I think I can mold into a woman exactly like me?"

At her brothers' identical horrified expressions, Lucy nearly laughed. But not before she wiggled up to a higher position on the pillows. She tried to look as professional as she could wearing a hospital gown and a bright fuchsia plaster cast.

"I accept," she said. "If the salary's right, I'd love to work at your offices." Where, she realized, her hot-pink cast would look right at home. Where, more important, she thought, she'd feel right at home.

Elise and John arrived on the receding wave of Claudia's perfume. With her family gathered around her, Lucy learned more about how the McMillan & Milano security personnel had controlled the crowd shortly after she'd fallen. John had called Carlo on the way to the hospital for all the details. Wrench, the rest of the Silver Bucket and their road crew had been arrested.

"The cops had to pull Carlo off the pyrotechnics guy," John said, sounding smug in that quiet way of his. "If Carlo hadn't been a former cop himself, they would probably have arrested him, too."

Then someone turned on the television and there was Lucy on the news. A video camera had caught her demanding Wrench to stop the show to calm the crowd. After she'd been pulled into the pit—the whole room had winced at the sight—the lead singer *had* cut the instruments with a slash of his hand. As the fans settled down, the camera had taken one last shot—and in it Lucy had seen a dark figure arrowing through the pack toward the place where she'd fallen.

Carlo found me, she thought. He would have been the one to pick her up and find her help. The hospital would be too much for him, she could understand that. But she knew, just knew, it was he who had picked her up from where she'd fallen and delivered her to the medical personnel.

Then he'd gone back to his dark corner, where he liked to observe life alone.

Later, the family left Lucy in her narrow bed. She tried to get out of bed to go with them, but the nursing staff insisted she stay a few more hours, and she was really too tired to argue. Her eyes closed as the dwarf drumming in her head finally put it on mute.

The room held dawn light when she opened her eyes again. Between the tall box of Godiva and the flower arrangement bristling with birds-of-paradise, she spotted Carlo's expressionless face.

"Hey," she murmured. "It's the right order. You come right after candy but before flowering plants."

A frown creased his forehead. "Shall I call a doctor?"

"Even an MD can't make a man better than chocolate."

"Your head injury...I'll come back later." He started to rise.

Blinking, she put out a hand. "You *are* here. I thought I was dreaming again. Last time it was a dwarf."

He settled back in the chair beside her bed, and she pushed at the table to see him more clearly. "It *is* you."

"It *is* me." His hand smoothed the thin blanket where it draped over the side of the mattress. "Are you okay?"

She remembered. "Better than okay. I have a new job! Claudia stopped by last night and made me an offer."

He nodded, as if taking that in. "Life is looking up, then."

"Yes." It was, she supposed. Because last night she'd thought things between her and Carlo were left so awkward that they could never be in a room together again. "You can go now, though," she said.

His gaze jumped to hers. What was that expression in his eyes? "You want me to go?"

"Well, um, whatever you feel like..." Lucy heard herself stepping into that familiar I'll-say-anything-he-wants role. Closing her eyes, she took a breath, then opened them again. "You're welcome to stay. It's nice to see you. But I know that hospitals make you uncomfortable."

"A lot of things make me uncomfortable," he muttered. He smoothed the blanket again, and she noticed the skinned knuckles. So she thought, he really had decked the pyrotechnics guy.

"You're hurt," she said, reaching out to brush his fingers with hers.

He caught her hand, then nodded at her cast. "*You're* hurt. I hate that you're hurt."

"I understand." And she did. It was how he'd changed after Patrick McMillan had died in his arms, under his watch. Carlo didn't want to care that deeply again and so...he didn't.

Carlo rubbed across her fingernails with the pad of his thumb, his gaze trained on their joined hands. "You're giving up too easy again, Lucy. You're willing to take less than you deserve. Less than you want."

Her heart started beating faster in her chest, as if it understood more than her mind. What did he mean? What was he saying?

"Pat's death put me in the shadows, Lucy. You lured me out."

"I'm not a trap." Her whisper was fierce. "I never meant to trap you." And if he didn't want to...to care for her, then she wasn't going to let it ruin her life.

"Still, I couldn't resist all the sticky sweetness."

That had her thinking about sex. About chocolate whipped cream and hot, intimate kisses. "Not fair."

"All right." His voice sounded strained. "But Lucy, just don't tell me that it's too late. Not now that I've stepped into your light."

She looked up. His face was still stone-hard, so expressionless it made her heart ache. "Too late for what?"

"For you to tell me again what you want?"

Oh, talk about traps. Her heart's speed went up another notch, but she still wasn't sure what he was getting at. She only knew she wasn't going to live a life where she did all the giving and the pleasing and the telling.

"So I have to take all the risk, is that it? You want me to jump and then you'll decide if the water's fine?"

He was silent a long minute. Then his gaze met hers. He sighed. "Lucy Sutton, you are one tough woman."

Apparently he couldn't see the untough sting of tears in her eyes, because she had the sudden sense that everything was going to be all right.

Carlo brought her hand to his mouth and kissed each one of her fingers. "Here goes, baby. Don't blink, because I'm about to execute my best dive."

Lucy's heart leaped and beat soft butterfly wings that made it hard to breathe.

"I'm in love with you, Lucy. You don't know—or maybe you do—how much I didn't want to be in this place, because I thought experiencing those feelings would be my worst nightmare. That they'd make me vulnerable to the kind of pain I felt when Pat died, to the kind of pain I've seen on Germaine's face. It seemed so much easier, more comfortable, saner, never to want to do that…"

"Couple thing," she finished for him.

He squeezed her fingers. "But then…but then I saw you fall and my vision of a nightmare changed entirely. Never letting you know what you mean to me, never seeing you smile or laugh or even cry—why, baby, why are you crying?—would be so much, much more terrible."

Leaning across the mattress, he laid a soft kiss on her lips, taking a tear or two away with it. "There's no time to waste, Luce. I get that now. Will you be my light, my love, my hope for happily-ever-after?"

Later, Lucy would make him pay for proposing to her when she had bedhead and was wearing a faded hospital gown. Secretly she would always think it was the most perfect moment in her entire life.

Later, Carlo would apologize profusely when she complained. Loudly, he would always tell her—truthfully—it was the most perfect moment of his entire life.

* * * * *

Look for LAST WOLF WATCHING
by Rhyannon Byrd—the exciting conclusion in
the BLOODRUNNERS miniseries
from Silhouette Nocturne.

Follow Michaela and Brody on their
fierce journey to find the truth and
face the demons from the past,
as they reach the heart of the battle
between the Runners and the rogues.

Here is a sneak preview of book three,
LAST WOLF WATCHING.

Michaela squinted, struggling to see through the impenetrable darkness. Everyone looked toward the Elders, but she knew Brody Carter still watched her. Michaela could feel the power of his gaze. Its heat. Its strength. And something that felt strangely like anger, though he had no reason to have any emotion toward her. Strangers from different worlds, brought together beneath the heavy silver moon on a night made for hell itself. That was their only connection.

The second she finished that thought, she knew it was a lie. But she couldn't deal with it now. Not tonight. Not when her whole world balanced on the edge of destruction.

Willing her backbone to keep her upright, Michaela Doucet focused on the towering blaze of a roaring bonfire that rose from the far side of the clearing, its orange flames burning with maniacal zeal against the inky-black curtain of the night. Many of the Lycans had already shifted into their preternatural shapes, their fur-covered bodies standing like monstrous shadows at the edges of the forest as they waited with restless expectancy for her brother.

Her nineteen-year-old brother, Max, had been attacked by a rogue werewolf—a Lycan who preyed upon humans for food. Max had been bitten in the attack, which meant he was no longer human, but a breed of creature that existed between the two worlds of man and beast, much like the Bloodrunners themselves.

The Elders parted, and two hulking shapes emerged from the trees. In their wolf forms, the Lycans stood over seven feet tall, their legs bent at an odd angle as they stalked forward. They each held a thick chain that had been wound around their inside wrists, the twin lengths leading back into the shadows. The Lycans had taken no more than a few steps when they jerked on the chains, and her brother appeared.

Bound like an animal.

Biting at her trembling lower lip, she glanced left, then right, surprised to see that others had joined her. Now the Bloodrunners and their family and friends stood as a united force against the Silvercrest pack, which had yet to accept the fact that something sinister was eating away at its foundation—something that would rip down the protective walls that separated their world from the humans'. It occurred to Michaela that loyalties were being announced tonight—a separation made between those who would stand with the Runners in their fight against the rogues and those who blindly supported the pack's refusal to face reality. But all she could focus on was her brother. Max looked so hurt...so terrified.

"Leave him alone," she screamed, her soft-soled, black satin slip-ons struggling for purchase in the damp earth as she rushed toward Max, only to find herself lifted off the ground when a hard, heavily muscled arm clamped around her waist from behind, pulling her clear off her feet. "Damn it, let me down!" she snarled, unable to take her eyes off her brother as the golden-eyed Lycan kicked him.

Mindless with heartache and rage, Michaela clawed at the arm holding her, kicking her heels against whatever part of her captor's legs she could reach. "Stop it," a deep, husky voice grunted in her ear. "You're not helping him by losing it. I give you my word he'll survive the ceremony, but you have to keep it together."

"Nooooo!" she screamed, too hysterical to listen to reason. "You're monsters! All of you! Look what you've done to him! How dare you! *How dare you!*"

The arm tightened with a powerful flex of muscle, cinching her waist. Her breath sucked in on a sharp, wailing gasp.

"Shut up before you get both yourself and your brother killed. I will *not* let that happen. Do you understand me?" her captor growled, shaking her so hard that her teeth clicked together. "Do you understand me, Doucet?"

"Damn it," she cried, stricken as she watched one of the guards grab Max by his hair. Around them Lycans huffed and growled as they watched the spectacle, while others outright howled for the show to begin.

"That's enough!" the voice seethed in her ear. "They'll tear you apart before you even reach him, and I'll be damned if I'm going to stand here and watch you die."

Suddenly, through the haze of fear and agony and outrage in her mind, she finally recognized who'd caught her. *Brody*.

He held her in his arms, her body locked against his powerful form, her back to the burning heat of his chest. A low, keening sound of anguish tore through her, and her head dropped forward as hoarse sobs of pain ripped from her throat. "Let me go. I have to help him. *Please*," she begged brokenly, knowing only that she needed to get to Max. "Let me go, Brody."

He muttered something against her hair, his breath warm against her scalp, and Michaela could have sworn it was a single word.... But she must have heard wrong. She was too upset. Too furious. Too terrified. She must be out of her mind.

Because it sounded as if he'd quietly snarled the word *never*.

nocturne™

THE FINAL INSTALLMENT OF
THE BLOODRUNNERS TRILOGY

Last Wolf Watching

Runner Brody Carter has found his match in
Michaela Doucet, a human with unusual psychic powers.
When Michaela's brother is threatened, Brody becomes
her protector, and suddenly not only has to protect her
from her enemies but also from himself....

LOOK FOR

LAST WOLF WATCHING
BY

RHYANNON
BYRD

Available May 2008 wherever you buy books.

Dramatic and Sensual Tales of Paranormal Romance

www.eHarlequin.com   SN61786

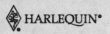
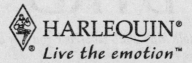

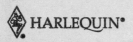

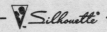

SPECIAL EDITION™

 THE WILDER FAMILY
Healing Hearts in Walnut River

Social worker Isobel Suarez was proud to work at Walnut River General Hospital, so when Neil Kane showed up from the attorney general's office to investigate insurance fraud, she was up in arms. Until she melted in his arms, and things got very tricky...

Look for

HER MR. RIGHT?

by

KAREN ROSE SMITH

Available May wherever books are sold.